Lyam's Journal

Alan Rogers

Copyright © 2008 by Alan Rogers

ISBN 0-7414-4505-0

Published by:

INFIƝITY
PUBLISHING.COM

1094 New DeHaven Street, Suite 100
West Conshohocken, PA 19428-2713
Info@buybooksontheweb.com
www.buybooksontheweb.com
Toll-free (877) BUY BOOK
Local Phone (610) 941-9999
Fax (610) 941-9959

Printed in the United States of America

Printed on Recycled Paper

Published December 2008

Lyam's Journal

Tuesday

Sitting in the kitchen, I look out the window trying to forget about an average day at work. The wind is blowing hard enough to cause the grass in my yard to sway, but the hairs on my arms remain stationary. I can taste the anger building up inside me, which usually overflows into some type of violent action, but as I keep my gaze fixed upon the oscillating grass, serenity overwhelms me.

During my youth, if I could manage to write down my thoughts during these episodes, my anger was assuaged, but using the bunny's blood for ink made my mom upset. The rabbit drained out faster than the kid next door, and was easier to control.

Today seems like as good a time as any to start keeping a journal. This will help clarify my thoughts, like butter. The medications can cause my eyesight to blur, making it difficult to write, but this will not deter me.

It will not be a diary, they are for pussies and punks, and I am neither. This will be my private journal, for my eyes only, unless someone else wants to read it. In order to prevent the police from making connections, my entries will specify the days, but not the dates. If you are going to catch me, it will take a little work.

It has begun to rain outside, and the pink rash on my left arm looks like it might be spreading. The skin inflammation erupted without any warning during the drive home from work. Perhaps acupuncture would cure the rash, but pins make me nervous even though the bank makes me have one.

My lovely wife is bogged down on the living room sofa watching the Wheel of Fortune, unaware of my arms condition. Her name is Mary and I will follow her anywhere, except the bathroom. Her short stature makes it easy for me to track her.

Our cat is rubbing its head against my legs which means she wants to be brushed. She is a gray striped tiger cat, but domesticated. Her name is Scooter, and she craves attention unless she is moody. When that happens, it forces me to adjust her diet. After lightly scratching my rash with her bristle brush, I begin the process of combing out her fur.

When cleaning off her brush, I save the fur in zip lock bags and store them in the closet. When I retire from my job, the bags will be weighed and set on fire.

Pulling a small clump of Scooter's hair from the brush, I hold it to my nose, and it reeks of dried blood. The odor induces my hunger, and I want to run out for a sandwich, but I never leave the house on Mondays after 7:30 p.m. There are rules in life even I must obey.

Suddenly, I remember today is Tuesday and it's not necessary for me to be confined, but it's still raining, so going for a sandwich is out of the question. There are chemicals within the rain that cause certain body parts to shrink.

Mary wants to know what I'm writing, but I pretend not to hear the query and her attention quickly returns to the television. My wife has always respected my privacy, causing me to wonder what has provoked this invasive question. At this juncture, she's starting to make me feel uncomfortable, like when Uncle Ed touched my penis.

I have never asked Mary why she likes kale, and she does not need to know where the bodies are buried in our yard. That's the secret to a happy marriage, not the shit Oprah tries to sell you.

The rash on my arm has faded away, Mary is finished watching the Wheel, and now she's cooking supper.

If it's time to eat, why do I have an erection?

Wednesday

As my wife and I are watching the Nightly News, heavy rain begins cascading off our roof, causing me to turn up the volume. The news anchor's hair seems to be soaking wet, and I wonder if our roof is leaking. After checking the ceiling and making sure my clothes are dry, there's no evidence of rain water seeping into our home. Mary is reclining on the couch, and her soft ebony skin glows invitingly in the lamplight. It's a great relief to see that she remains moisture free.

On the news President Bush is explaining about his war and the importance of sand. I have observed the President on television many times, but have never seen his feet. My set is only 28 inches tall.

Marching to the closet, I grab the tape measure and stretch it out the length of my leg. My inseam is 38 inches long, but if my feet were missing it would be less. Mary is scrutinizing my movements, but she asks no questions. She trusts me completely, and I love her for that, even if it's slightly naive on her part.

The President is striding toward his helicopter, but he doesn't appear to limp. The Marine guard glances down toward the ground as the President approaches. Does the soldier wonder why the President doesn't have feet? Is that jelly on the remote? I need to concentrate, like orange juice.

God has blessed me with two feet, and this makes me grateful. If the President had feet, would he dare to wear sneakers with orange laces? Agent orange contributed to the death of many veterans and George Bush is a veteran, loosely speaking.

I wonder how many people have lost their feet in wars, and why the sneakers still cost so much. Does anybody even know what a cobbler is?

Living in the country has its benefits because people don't notice my feet. Country folks aren't cognizant of much, and rarely visit the dentist.

I glance furtively across the room to see if Mary is watching me, but she seems mesmerized by the television. Some days, I worry about mind control, and there are other times when I can sense eyes watching me. There's a cow eye in my freezer sealed inside a zip lock bag.

I don't dare to ask Mary why the President doesn't have feet because she has a pair. One of her toes is crooked, like some crows claw, and she's sensitive about it.

President Bush continues smirking as he responds to the reporter's questions. He grins like a mentally deficient person, and it makes me wonder who dropped the baby.

He's babbling on and on about lowering taxes for the affluent. It makes me curious, how this will affect the price of grapefruits. Many years ago, when my young body was desperate, I arranged to have a sexual liaison with a grapefruit. Mary doesn't know about my affair with the fruit, and it's best to leave it that way. You should always remember to steam heat before using.

How many people have lost their feet due to disease? My grandfather had gangrene, causing him to lose both his legs, which included his feet. Gangrene smells like waffles in the toaster on Easter morning. Where do hospitals dispose of the feet they remove?

President Bush has a dog trotting beside him, and the mutt looks lonely. Wasn't there a Presidential pet named Sock's? I wear a sock after sex in order not to unnecessarily frighten people.

If I owned a dog, he could sleep at my feet, and this makes me question where the President's dog slumbers.

Mary wants to know what I'm writing, but I don't respond. There should be no secrets between a husband and wife. This little journal will be my secret. She smiles at me, and I grin back, easily placating her curiosity. This is almost like real life, and it must be great fun to have me as a husband.

It is an honor to have feet when the President does not. President Roosevelt spent some of his days in a wheelchair, which makes me wonder if they will allow you to be President if you have feet. My kitty has four feet, but if I were to amputate two, what would she become?

Grabbing the tape, I measure my leg again, and this time its 37 inches. Are my feet wearing away? How many more miles do my soles have left?

President Bush waves to the crowd of reporters as he boards the helicopter, but I don't think he understands the news is over.

Friday

Today, the package I have been waiting for all week arrived in the mail. The mailman must have delivered it, but I didn't see him. Actually, I have never seen the mailman, and at times this makes me nervous, but not today.

My Littman stethoscope is finally here, and there will be no more sharing ear wax. Ear wax smells like cancer, and my mom had cancer, but I never looked inside her ears.

Removing the stethoscope from the box, I begin putting it together. Assembling items is not a natural behavior for me, I prefer to tear things apart. The rubber components smell like Saranac Lake, where mom took me to camp when I was eight years old.

Father Francis was the camp administrator, and he would take us swimming almost every day. "We won't be needing any trunk's boys," he would say. The water was cold, but Father Francis was warm. This proves how alarming contrast can be.

Placing the stethoscope over my heart, I hear thub bum, thub bum. The beat reminds me of a salsa band. Last year, I bet on a horse named Thurbum at Saratoga, and he came in seventh, costing me ten dollars. The horse wasn't fast, but my heart kept on beating.

Scooter seems to be exhibiting some interest in the new instrument. Cats are naturally curious animals, and that can be dangerous. Placing the stethoscope against Scooter's furry side, I attempt to listen to her heart, but the multitude of sounds leave me unable to ascertain one from the other. She probably has worms. Without her being aware, I slip a librium into her water bowl. I will need to check her heart rate again in thirty minutes.

My instrument did not arrive with a storage case, but under the sink there's an old ice chest with rust-colored stains inside. The stains don't wash out, but the stethoscope fits nicely.

Taking my new toy outside, I search in vain for a patient. There's a cricket on the deck, but when I attempt to listen to the insect's heart, no sounds come through the device. I really need to get my hearing checked. Some yucky material is smeared on the instrument's bell, and the cricket is not moving. This type of thing has happened before, but the memory eludes me.

After scraping the viscous fluid from the bell with my fingers, I return inside the house so Scooter can lick them clean. My life has always been about putting others first, especially when a train is coming.

Returning outside, I place the stethoscope against the trunk of the oak tree growing beside my deck. Once again, there's nothing to hear. The company may have mailed me a defective instrument.

My next door neighbor is driving by, and I take time out to wave. God loves courtesy. He turns his head, as if he did not see me and drives on. When he returns home, I will offer him a friendship lesson. His name is Wilbert Sandgart, and he's a private person. I live in a small town where most of the citizens are named Wilbert. I wonder if their hearts all sound the same.

My bladder is bursting, so I run back inside the house to urinate. Sometimes I will piss outside, but not when the wind is blowing.

In the bathroom, I place the stethoscope over the tip of my third nipple and listen carefully. Thub bum, thub bum. Apparently my hearing has been restored.

The bald headed man in the mirror requests my help

without moving his lips. There are three swollen nipples on his chest also, and this oddity makes me nervous. What are the odds?

Scooter is standing in the doorway watching me, but she seems unaware of the guy in the mirror. I wink at her, and she runs down the hallway.

Checking in the mirror, I make sure there's nothing in my eye.

Sunday

This is my day off from work, and despite the relaxed atmosphere at home, I feel anxious. This can be remedied by taking two more of the blue pills.

Looking out the kitchen window, I notice there's a crow resting comfortably in the yard. Do crows sleep on their sides? It's too early for me to have the answers to these tough questions.

I need to use the bathroom, but don't have to raise my hand anymore. The bathroom mirror can be a scary thing when other people appear in it, but it's a relief to see myself. My bald head houses two of the most malevolent eyes ever seen, other than my fathers.

When I return to the kitchen, the crow remains in the yard. For some reason this reminds me of Mary's parents. Do crows normally sleep during the day? The encyclopedia is quite informative, but it doesn't have any details about sleep habits. This is disturbing, and I make a mental note to write the publishing company.

Scooter is pretending to sleep, but something tells me she wants to see the crow. Snuggling her up into my arms we go outside, one man and his bundle of joy. Years ago, I was not allowed outside without restraints and escorts. It taught me to appreciate my freedom. Scooter tries to escape my grasp, in anticipation of the adventure that lies ahead.

Do crows blink? What is West Nile Virus? I place

Scooter on the ground approximately five inches from the crow, this is the appropriate viewing distance for wild animals. She declines the inspection, and scampers back toward the house.

I understand how animals can be easily confused, so I grab her by the scruff of the neck and carry her back. I firmly press her face into the crows shiny feathers. Scooter's fur puffs up, and she arches her back, but the crow doesn't respond. Do crows have spines? This may call for further investigation.

My lower back is throbbing from supporting Scooter's fat ass all this time. I decide the crow is the dearly departed.

The kitty and I go back inside the house to eat lunch. Did I wash my hands?

Monday

This morning the crow remains in the yard, and it's still there when I return from work. The bird appears to have increased in size, and I wonder who delivered food. There's an empty pizza box lying on the ground across the street. Do crows know about Jenny Craig? Are they sensitive? Why didn't I pay more attention in school?

I try not to stare at the crow, but the birds piercing black eyes seem to track my every move. Are my pants unzipped? The crow's eyes shine like my dad's shoes on church day.

There's a faint aroma in the air which reminds me of bacon frying. When I was three years old, my Uncle Ed locked me in his cellar for several months and fed me bacon. There were no crows in the basement, but pigs with huge feet still haunt my dreams. Can crows dream? Not this one, I bet.

Mary has wandered outside, and is leaning over the deck railing. She questions my activity, and I explain to her about making a documentary for the nature channel. My wife does not understand how much I love animals. Are birds animals?

During supper, I admire the crow through the window, and the chicken is delicious.

Tuesday

Last night was bitter cold, but the weather does not seem to affect the crow. I don't appreciate the chilly temperatures we have in the Northeast, but I do enjoy ice cream. Crows can't eat ice cream because their claws are unable to hold the cone.

Throwing my light blue jacket over my shoulders, I stroll outside to examine the crow, and my attention is drawn to the birds three-toed feet. Racing back inside the house, I quickly count the number of toes on my cat. Scooter has three toes also. There are five toes on each of my feet, and this disparity makes me feel abandoned. This could be remedied by amputating two toes from each of my feet, but who will determine which ones.

Scooter has no opinion, the decision is made not to cut, and my kitty purrs approval.

Mary doesn't like blood spilled on the kitchen floor, except for one time.

Wednesday

I woke up early this morning, and left Mary snoring in bed while I went to see if the crow was still sleeping. From the kitchen window observatory, I'm able to ascertain that the bird remains stationary. I wave at the crow, but there's no response.

Scooter is awake, and seems to be interested in my

activities. I hold her up to the window, enabling her to survey the yard. She playfully tries to pull back away from me, but due to my vast knowledge of animal behavior, I understand she needs my help. I press her furry head firmly against the glass, until she yowls with pleasure.

From the bedroom, Mary is demanding to know what's going on. While humming a Marvin Gaye song, I inform her that Scooter is hungry. I wrap my fingers gently around her throat, and the annoying clamor ceases. Was it the cat's throat or my wife's? Scooter's eyes bulge in thanks.

Putting on my lucky blue jacket, I run outside to commune with the crow. Hundreds of flies have gathered around the bird's campground, but the critter doesn't seem aware of the insects. Getting down on my hands and knees, I gently touch the bird with one finger, and it causes the feathers to twitch. Could it have been some type of optical illusion? Does David Copperfield ever use crows?

The nasty buzzing flies are crawling all over the crow in haphazard fashion. The bird's dignity may be at stake. The incessant drone issuing from the insects sounds like Lyfe Jennings on his first album. Placing my face close to the crow, I inhale deeply, and am rewarded with the fragrance of spicy gummy bears.

My neighbor is watching me from his living room window, causing me to cut short the visit with my feathered friend. This is a quiet neighborhood.

Thursday

This morning, a flock of crows has flown in to visit with my crow. Perhaps they are going to conduct a meeting, or hold a convention.

They are poking at my bird with their beaks, trying in vain to wake him up. The visitors appear to be eating something, but I'm unable to perceive a food source. Do you think Jeffrey Dahmer ever studied crows?

Scooter seems to be missing in action this morning. Sometimes people lose things, but I have a third nipple that can always be found.

My neighbor is furtively making his way across my yard toward the crow, while carrying a garbage bag and a shovel. Wilbert is probably coming over to borrow something.

Ever since his dog died, my neighbor tries his best to avoid me. It's encouraging to see him overcome his antisocial tendencies, but it makes me angry that he has ventured into my yard without permission.

I step outside, and greet him with a smile on my face. It's what good neighbors do. My route has brought me to an area of the yard between Wilbert and his intended destination. We stand face to face, and he averts his gaze to the ground.

Wilbert's wife passed away six months ago and his dog died a few days later. There may be a hidden meaning to these events, but due to my rage it escapes me.

Constructively, I remind my neighbor of the recent losses that have been directed his way. His face dissolves into tears, as a whimpering sound escapes from his mouth. He hastily retreats inside his house. The curtains behind his window waver, alerting me that he continues to watch this event transpire from the safety of his home.

As a good neighbor, my desire is for Wilbert to see my softer side. I smile and wave toward his window. He retired from Sears last year, and I think it would be a good idea if he found himself a hobby. I pat the crow lovingly on its malformed head, and go back inside my house.

Scooter has returned from her secret hiding place, and she appears no worse for wear. I pour some food in her bowl, and make myself a cup of coffee. We guard the yard together, one man and his kitty securing their property.

Wilbert does not return outside. He's a loner, and you have to keep an eye on those people.

There's a feather floating in my coffee cup, and Scooter has started to lick herself with wild abandon. Before hurting my back, I was able to perform the very same feat, and it was quite rewarding.

Pasta for lunch.

Friday

When I woke up, the crow was gone, and it makes me thankful to be alive in such a magical world.

Saturday

I have decided its time to buy a new car. There's nothing like the fresh smell of leather to revive memories of my father's belt. My dad was a huge man, but he's been brought down to size. His name is Bud, like the beer.

While driving to the auto mall, I remain silent and respectful in order not to disturb my wife. Mary is not permitted to drive unless she's by herself. Guardrails can cause grievous bodily harm, worse than dad's belt.

Mary's eyes are closed, and she seems totally relaxed during the drive. With my right hand, I reach across the console and caress circles on her thigh. Her perfume fills the vehicle with the fragrance of wild flowers. Dead people appreciate receiving flowers, but my wife does not. She firmly instructs me to cease my activities, and places my hand on the steering wheel.

The Ford dealership is open for business when we arrive, but there's no water. We begin our self guided tour around the lot, and I admire the shiny paint on the new cars. The autos have been heavily waxed, and the glare causes me to squint in order to avoid injuring my retinas.

A salesman is stalking us, smiling and holding out his hand for me to shake. His oversized head has a gaping hole full of horse teeth, which makes me decline to shake his hand, but Mary does. When we return home, I will speak with her about good touch, bad touch.

The salesman's name is Paul, and he recommends taking a vehicle out for a test drive. This seems like a great idea, and Mary makes the prudent choice to follow my lead. I love my wife.

After driving the Ford Taurus off the lot, it's not long before the urge to run over something invades my world view. Once I was empty inside, but now I am full. God is good.

There's a child riding a bicycle less than fifty feet in front of me, and this demands a quick decision on my part. I look at my wife for some sign of approval, but her eyes deny my request.

Having learned from previous experience to obey my spouse, I slowly back the car off the lawn. I'm careful not to disturb the grass in case there are people nearby who have allergies.

The agile child has run inside the house, leaving the bicycle behind. The missed opportunity makes me feel nauseous.

I drive rather quickly back to the dealership where Paul is waiting for us with a moronic grin plastered on his face. There's an intense desire in my heart to slice his lips off, and hang them from my belt. He has extremely hairy arms, and I wonder how they feel when wet. The man is causing the snake in my stomach to twist.

Coral snakes are beautiful reptiles, but they are venomous. Several years ago, at a birthday party, I filled a piñata with them. Swing harder children. The hospital had antivenin, but disappointments will never restrain me. Perseverance is a virtue.

Paul guides us inside the musty building to his office, where I make an offer, and he counters with one of his own. This is annoying, like when my father tickled me with the mop. I write the number on a yellow sticky note, and paste it on top of his head.

He feigns the need to check this price with his boss,

and boldly struts away. He made no offer to take us with him, and I consider this behavior rude. Reaching into my pocket, I am reassured by the presence of the guitar string.

Paul waltzes into the office, and offers us coffee. I didn't drive to Schenectady for a fucking cup of coffee, I came to purchase a car.

Mary accepts the beverage despite my warning. Doesn't she remember what happened at Jonestown? Poisons dissolve easier in coffee than in Kool Aid. She sips the hot coffee and appears to be fine, but experience has taught me not to take chances. I remain vigilant. Many years ago at a carnival, I took one chance and was taught a valuable lesson. Clowns wear big shoes.

Paul informs us that his boss will sell for one price, but I prefer the number previously written on the sticky note. It's my age in dog years multiplied by fifty. This number has produced excellent results in the past. This time, I inscribe the number on Paul's shirt. It's possible our salesman may be mildly retarded. Paul maintains that his boss is a tough nut to crack, and it's becoming increasingly difficult to conceal my hatred for the man. My elimination mode could be easily accessed, but Mary shakes her head negatively. I sense Paul is attempting to provoke me.

I excuse myself to use the bathroom because pissing helps me relax. It's like perpetuating an orgasm.

Paul's boss is sitting in an office across from the men's room, and this seems like a golden opportunity. The voice that resides behind my left ear whispers the execution command, and divulges Paul's middle initial.

The big boss is a frail elderly man who shakes uncontrollably as he studies the papers on his desk. This could be the old buzzard's lucky day. Helping the aged is a gift God has blessed me with, it's like helping them across the street, only the distance is further.

In the bathroom, the urinal is sparkling clean, but my heart is not. While washing my hands, I wonder where my guitar string went, and why my fingers are sore.

Despite not having a map, I return to the office where

Paul and Mary are waiting. Where's Peter? Paul wants to know if we are serious about buying the Taurus. This guy has turned out to be a fucking idiot.

There's something different about Mary's appearance, and it forces me to check her pants for stains, but I don't notice any.

Paul declares the need to consult with his boss one last time, but he returns quickly, looking confused. Apparently, his boss has disappeared without informing anyone, and I have a hunch he won't be coming back.

In spite of the salesman's incompetence, we make the deal, and the new Taurus will be ready for delivery in three days. It would be nice to take Paul's teeth home with me, but you can't always get what you want. Our new car is blue, but I would have preferred flesh color.

Monday

While driving on my way to work, reality smacks me in the face. My job sucks. This should have been self evident, after stepping on a bug when coming out of my house this morning. The insect's blood was green, and it spelled Retire Now on my deck.

The trip to work takes me through the small town of Ballston Spa, where God seems to have put the slow people in a cluster. The good citizens of this town always keep an eye out for me, and they recognize my car by sight. Small town folks tend to make me nervous. There's not much to keep their mind's active.

My brother had an accident in a small town, and they took him to a rehabilitation hospital where they helped him walk again. I never went to visit him during his stay because the food at the hospital was not very appetizing. Ralph likes donuts, but I don't.

I am employed at a drug rehab, where we teach people life skills, even though most of the patients don't have one. We teach them how to abuse drugs productively, by substituting their drugs for our drugs so the pharmaceutical companies can make money instead of Flaco.

It can be depressing work, but nobody has the right to be happy all the time, unless you are an Exxon executive. There are days I feel like crying, but this is not one of them.

There's security where I work, but this does not signify we are safe. They hire our security guards from the local retirement home. How is grown man who wears a diaper going to protect me?

After pulling into the parking lot, I jump out of the car, and follow my fellow employees through the door that leads to despair. The scent of bleach and urine wafting down the hallway alerts me to arrival at my place of employment.

Drugs are against the law, and my grandmother died with a pocket full of raisins, but not from substance abuse. If a person abuses drugs, should they be considered a criminal, or an addict? Should we try to rehabilitate the addicts, or would it be more efficient to kill them before they kill themselves?

Ralph was always able to answer my tough questions, but my brother isn't available. He's able to walk fairly well now, and doesn't consider himself disabled even though he retains an awkward hitch in his hip.

Ralph tries to maintain his sense of humor, but he never really learned how to laugh. I believe laughter is the best medicine. My brother did smile once when a dog bit me. It's not wise to push a straw into an animal's ear.

The crackheads who come for treatment claim to be disabled and depressed. I think if they really want to understand what depression is, they should try working here. There are moments in everybody's lifetime when they feel depressed, but it's just one part of daily life, so deal with it.

When I was three years old, my Uncle Ed locked me in a cellar for almost a year after he became possessive. If he had introduced me to illicit drugs instead of feeding me hickory smoked bacon, would an addict be writing this journal?

Some of our patients are on methadone maintenance, which makes it seem like something they are still working on. There are patients who smoke crack, but won't eat pork. If a pork chop is tender, I will gnaw that pig to the bone, but I have never smoked crack. Why is it, this makes me feels guilty?

We have a free cafeteria, but most of the employees who display even a moderate level of intelligence don't eat there. Two of the guys that work on the serving line pick their noses constantly, but not when the inspectors show up.

The state inspectors are pleasant folks, and one of them is a woman who has a huge set of thighs. My mom had muscular thighs from standing long hours while cutting down trees, but she never inspected our food.

We take blood pressures here, but the numbers always come out even, and this seems odd. They have white towels throughout the building, but nobody ever surrenders. Some of the nurses drop pills on the floor for me to discover. It's part of the employee's assistance program, and they are safe to ingest if you brush them off first.

When I test my urine, the dipstick always reads positive for several substances. This helps me relate to our patients.

Last week, I tested Scooter's urine because her pupils were pinpoint. Trust has to be earned, and then cherished.

Do two geese make a flock? What makes a group? They talk all day long about finding recovery here, but my only desire is to find my way home.

Do they have drug and alcohol rehabs in Bogota? Why do the cars in the parking lot all face the same way? If your car is parked facing in the opposite direction will it cause you to relapse? You pray facing Mecca, why can't I park facing Malta?

There are days, I just want to hide in my car until my shift is over, but responsibility does not allow me to do that. You can thank my mom for teaching me about dependableness.

Wednesday

Another day here at work, and the gum is still stuck on the window. Eight years, three months, two days, seven hours, and fifty minutes, no fifty-one. The time keeps on changing, and I have no control over it.

The gum has been on the window ever since I started working here, allowing us to share many experiences over the years. We are close, but not in a sexual way, it's a spiritual bond we have.

The gum is stuck on the stairwell window outer surface. It's located between the first and second floors, and the window does not open. It makes me wonder how the gum managed to get out there. After Uncle Ed died, I peeled open one of his eyes, but he didn't see me.

The window has never been broken to my knowledge, and the gum retains its privacy. I wonder if there's any flavor left. It's raining fiercely, but the gum maintains its grip. This revives memories of clasping onto mom's leg as she held my head underwater, despite the fact I wasn't thirsty. The gum's tenacity is admirable. Why won't it fall off?

The window is cool to the touch, but when I touch myself there is warmth. Contrasting temperatures have always interested me. The gum can't be felt through the window, but can it sense me?

The gum's surface is gray and wrinkled, the same way mom's hand looked when she pushed my head under the water. My mother was sensitive about aging, so I never mentioned wrinkles. She returned the favor by telling the neighbors not to feed me.

I feel drawn to stare at the gum even though it's not polite. It's glued to the glass, but I have never worn glasses. Life is filled with so many mysteries.

My name is being paged on the overhead speaker, and this always annoys me. How does the person on the page know my name, and what do they want? Don't they understand I'm busy?

Sally was a woman who always knew my name, and I wonder if she's been hired. She was a bipolar hooker, and we used to have sex during her manic phase. It was similar to riding the roller coaster at Lake George.

Sometimes, I will cry and cut myself superficially, but never when the gum can see me. Cutting can be a great conversation starter at family reunions.

I shave my head every other day, but have never cut myself while doing this. This is something to be proud of in a world full of despair. Peanut butter and jelly, raisins and ants, cold steel and warm flesh, some things are just meant to be together.

The gum is calm, and this reassures me that everything is going turn out all right. In the winter, the gum seems to stiffen in the cold, but still it clings to the window. Do lepers get frostbite?

Occasionally, my brother's face will appear etched in the gum, but the impression is inaccurate. Ralph has teeth, but the gum does not. My brother also has a mole on his back that's shaped like the state of Illinois. He has traveled to Chicago three times, but never to Wrigley Field.

My boss has found me loitering in the stairwell, admiring the gum. She doesn't see the gum, and I'm not inclined to point it out to her. There's no point.

She wants to know if I heard my page, but I remain in a state of confusion, which is nowhere near Illinois. My boss's name is Tina, and thorny questions are her specialty. Why does she stand that way on the stairs? Is she being seductive? How difficult would it be to push her?

While remaining polite, my defenses are on red alert. Tina has a master's degree in entrapment. My mouth smiles, but my eyes don't.

She constructively reminds me about some paperwork needing to be filed. I usually do what people tell me, unless there are grounds not to. Reasonableness exudes from me. Maybe this is my opportunity to become the employee of the month.

After lunch, I return to the stairwell for some private

time with my friend. The gum does not eat lunch, or any other meal. I wish it were possible to chew the gum, to absorb the wisdom.

The weather has changed, and it's starting to warm up, but the gum still hangs on. There's a blue magic marker in my pocket, but it's not really magic. Would the gum be more comfortable if the window was tinted blue?

With nobody in the stairwell, I stretch my penis to the window. Perhaps the gum can feel me, or maybe it can't, but at least I tried.

The window is shaded blue, my car is blue, and Uncle Ed's dead lips were blue. I like this color.

Saturday

The best hot dogs in the world are Hebrew National because God has blessed them. My wife and I are going on a trip to the casino today. Mary is like the lamb, she goes everywhere I go, and watching out for her is my duty.

Our destination is the Mohegan Sun Casino, and I wonder if we will see any Indians when we arrive. I am not Sikh. The casino is located on a reservation, but I have none.

It's a tedious drive, and I pray along the way. God is important in my life. There are deer parts strewn all along the side of the highway, heads, legs, and torsos. What has caused this gruesome destruction? Does it matter? The deer seem to have fallen apart.

I pull off the highway into the rest area, not because I'm tired, but to satisfy my blood lust. Usually, I'm such a peaceful man, it must be all the deer blood.

Did David feel this way when he hacked off Goliath's head? There are no stones on the ground to guide me. I ask God, but there's no answer. He must be busy, and I hope he has call waiting.

I walk to the edge of the highway to stretch out my legs, and there's a deer smeared on the shoulder of the road.

Not a whole one, just entrails and legs. The guts spell out my first name, but its spelled wrong. No spelling bee winner this year.

I was given a simple name at birth, but everybody wants to put an extra L in Lyam. Fortunately, I have one knife in my pocket, seven more in the car, and many more at home. Mary calls me a collector.

I cut loose the extra L from the rest of the intestines, and intercede with God on behalf of the poor dead deer. God agrees to my request.

I notice Mary praying inside the car. Her eyes are closed, and she's drooling against the window. I hope she intends to clean up the mess. She's a good Christian, and I love her more than life itself. Then again, maybe not that much.

The sight of her drool sliding down the glass is making me aroused, hard as stone. Please Lord not here, not now. I pray for God's forgiveness, while placing the entrail L inside the car trunk. It will be food for my kitty when we get back home. Scooter can be finicky, so I bless the food.

There's no traffic as I urinate beside the car, but I sense God watching. He has seen me naked many times, and has probably been impressed. Adam and Eve were naked, but neither of them had an L in their names. God knows about the hairy mole on my side. God knows everything. Jesus loves me, and I love Jesus.

It's amazing how prayer can change things. My blood rage is gone, but my shoes are wet, and this is peculiar.

I slide back into the car, and drive on. Mary stirs next to me, and I assume she has completed her prayers. She wants to know if we are there yet, and I fear she has gone blind. Jesus heals blind people. I pray, and after turning to face my wife, her eyes light up with love for me. I have witnessed a miracle, and it causes me to praise God silently. During the last few years, I have learned to worship quietly, in order not to frighten people.

We finally arrive at the casino, and I manage to park my own car. I'm a big boy. Gambling is a sin, so I don't gamble, you can never win.

Inside the casino, there are lights and noises, bells and hammers. It reminds me of the hospital where they held me in restraints for many years. They pulled me into the shape of a star, and it was a star that showed the way to the baby Jesus. Jesus was at the hospital with me, but when they let me go, He stayed.

Mary loves the slot machines, and I'm attracted to slots, but not machines. Five years ago, I touched the handle of a slot machine, and it was warm and rubbery like a foreskin. I asked God to forgive me, and after keeping me waiting for a few moments, He agreed to my request.

You should never play craps, unless you are a sinner. The Roman's cast lots for the garments of Jesus. Did they have dice? You can roll snake eyes, but I was born with snake eyes, and you can't roll me.

It's getting late in the afternoon, and my stomach is growling with hunger. God is the great provider. As Mary and I make our way to the buffet, we can't help noticing how many fat people are in line.

Mary informs me, they are large people and can't help it, but I respond by telling her that they are fat-fuck's, and gluttony is a sin. My compassion allows me to pray for the fat folks, so Jesus can help them. Sometimes God will let me trim the fat, but not today. The knife is in my pocket, and it gives me comfort. Jesus will be your comfort in the storm.

Before we begin eating, I hold my wife's hand, and together we bless the food. Mary is trying to tell me something, but her mouth is moving without any sounds coming out. This does not cause me any great alarm. I don't need conversation, I need ejaculation. After eating a cannoli, my ears are opened. Is God Italian?

Mary is having fun, and if you are not careful, fun can be sinful. God has rules, and we try to live an orderly life.

Returning to the slot machines, Mary sits down and resumes playing while I observe. A cute woman wearing very little clothes offers us drinks, and I accept one.

Drunkenness is a sin, but I'm not drunk.

Mary keeps putting money into the machine, and sometimes it comes back, just like herpes. Jesus kicked the moneychanger's ass, and I wonder if the Lord would like me to slice a few people.

A scruffy obese man sits down next to Mary, and begins to play his machine, while belching last weeks fritters into the air. My stomach is rolling, but Mary does not seem bothered by the moldy smell.

The man is wearing a dirty T - shirt, and wins on his first spin. There's a stain on his right shoulder, and I can't remember if Jesus was right-handed. Please don't hit me with the ruler again.

The stain begins to quiver, and it tells me to be a good servant. Can I please use the knife? God says no, and God knows best. Could God be Robert Young?

The stain is making me uncomfortable, our money is gone, and it's time to go home. We have made our first fruits offering for today. Lions ate the early Christians, but I am a missionary.

After starting the car, it seems like some fog has built up on the windshield. There's a dirty old shirt on the back seat, and I use it to wipe off the window.

It's dark out, and on the drive home I don't see any deer, but their eyes are watching.

Sunday

They charge me six dollars to drive into the Saratoga State Park. As a taxpayer, I own the park. Should I be able to get a refund? You can walk into the park for free. What does the state do with the six dollars they collect? Last year I bought a carpet.

The collector inside the booth looks like he could use a new pair of shoes. I give him ten dollars, and tell him to keep the change. I am a philanthropist. He informs me, they are not allowed to take money, but when I smile, he stuffs the extra cash in his pocket. State workers are very intuitive. My inner child is pleased, and it's wise not to make him angry.

After driving a few yards beyond the booth, I park in one of the pull outs without anyone noticing. Mary and I stroll into the recreation area holding hands. We are always together until the Reaper splits us, or until my wife becomes rabid. There's no foam bubbling from her mouth this morning.

Walking in the park can be amusing because the place is huge, and there are plenty of places to hide. I like to watch the squirrels running through the grass, and sometimes I will smell the ground where they have been. Some people presume I'm nuts.

Squirrels love nuts, and they are extremely adept at hiding things. I enjoy hiding things too. Nobody has discovered the hiding places in my yard, but my hands get blisters, and the squirrel's paws don't.

There's a golf course within the park, and I can observe the golfers as we walk. You have to be aware of your surroundings at all times. When the golfers swing their clubs, huge divots are ripped loose from the ground. This makes me inflamed, but I don't scratch. The grass is innocent, and does not deserve to be treated in a disrespectful manner.

Sometimes, there are extra golf balls hidden near the greens, like an Easter egg hunt without the eggs. I snatch up the extra balls, and put them in my pants pocket. When I get home, my kitty will sniff them. The golfers will yell in my direction, and wave their arms in the air, apparently encouraging my endeavors.

Pulling up a few blades of grass from around one of the holes, I stuff them in my shirt pocket. Mary and I continue our walk. The music from her thighs rubbing together soothes my soul.

Joggers are streaking past us, arousing my desire to trip one, but I restrain myself. They might scratch me as they are falling. There are many infections in this world, and you have to be careful.

My chakra's are in alignment, and it helps me to maintain a greater level of self control. In prison they made me walk in line, at Disneyland they made me wait in line, proving life is a circle if you live long enough.

All the squirrels in the park appear similar, and I wonder about cloning. Which one was the original? I would ask Mary, but she demands my silence during our walks, so she can commune with nature. Maybe I should ask the park ranger.

There are samples of my semen at home, should cloning ever become popular. Most of the specimens are kept in old jars, but they are clean. Two samples are in Coke containers, and it's the real thing.

Two years ago, I gave one jar to the furnace repair-man, and he seemed surprised. There was no need to thank me, there's more where that came from. My hands are always sticky.

It's starting to get quite warm in the park, so we head back to the car before Mary starts sweating. She doesn't like her skin to be wet, unless it's a special occasion.

I lick the edge of the driver's side window before rolling it down. It enables the glass to slide easier. Mary chooses not to notice me.

During the drive home, I remove the grass from my shirt pocket and let it fly out the window. My heart is racing. A single blade of grass is stuck to my thumb, so I lick it off and swallow.

Can anyone still remember when they gave you green stamps with your gas?

The grass tastes like freedom.

Monday

I have not been able to sleep for the past three days, despite the relaxation techniques applied by my wife. The medication my doctor prescribed does not help, and it causes the hairs on my nipples to grow.

Exhaustion has overtaken me, and I just need to rest my eyes for one minute.....

The Parole Board is going to meet with me today. It's the third time I have stepped up, and twice before they have denied my freedom. Maybe this time they will have the good sense to let me go. Two words come to mind, what if? After being locked up for seven years, it's time for me to fly.

How can you be lonely in prison? There are tiers full of folks to keep you company. The Parole Board should not consider me a bad man, I just had one bad day. It was a worse day for the people left behind. I'm not an archaeologist, but the police found the bones hidden in the woods.

I sit on a hard wooden bench outside the room, waiting for the Board to call me. Waiting has never been a problem, I'm a patient hunter. There's a CO standing outside the door to the room where the decision about my freedom will be made. Thirst overwhelms me, and I would enjoy sticking an orange juicer in the CO's eye. He calls out my last name and number, as he opens the magic door. Someday, I will win the lottery with that number.

I saunter slowly into the room, giving them time to understand who's in charge. There's no rush, they have kept me waiting for seven fucking years. Two men and one woman are seated at a long metal table in the center of the room. I try to draw some meaning from the numbers, but fail.

The Board does not stand up when I enter the room, and this is rude. To show them how much prison has mellowed me, I let the offence slide. My therapist enters the room through a side door, gently guides me to a chair, and sits down beside me.

Trust is a wonderful thing, until it sucks all the life from your body. My therapist's name is Susan, and she smells like fresh milk and vinegar. I have learned to appreciate therapy, and I long for the opportunity to perform it naked.

The man sitting at the center of the table welcomes me to the Parole Board. He is respectful, and calls me Mr. Rogers. Nobody ever calls me Mister unless they want to fight. Despite my last name, I do not wear sweaters, and am not a Presbyterian. I did filet a Baptist during a picnic in 1970.

It's important to maintain eye contact with the speaker, unless you wear glasses. The pleasant man has a name tag that reads Mr. Barban. He demands to know what I have done to improve myself since the previous Parole Board.

Three answers to his question come to mind. 1) I have stopped eating potatoes in the mess hall. 2) I have looked inside myself by studying my feces. 3) I have killed some of the short people. I choose my answer carefully, and can read nothing from his expression as I respond.

The woman on the left side of the table takes her turn. Her name tag reads Ms. Pacer, and I wonder what the fuck Ms. means. She wants to know how I plan to manage my anger more appropriately, if they decide to release me.

My response is to explain about the anger management classes that were made available during my stay. Ms. Pacer is quite attractive with her pouting lips and olive skin. I attempt to touch my eye with the tip of my tongue, but if she's impressed her face doesn't give it away. The room seems to be getting warm, and it forces me to untie my shoes.

The last Board member is seated at the far end of the desk. He introduces himself as Mr. Torres. I wonder if he's an illegal, but I don't ask. He wants to know how I plan to retain employment. How the fuck am I supposed to know. The response issued from my mouth is much more sedate. Being able to control your emotions in stressful situations can be beneficial, thanks to anger management, and the haldol. The trustee I killed before breakfast was helpful in his own way.

I explain to Mr. Torres that I enjoy working with raw meat, and I might find employment as a butcher's apprentice.

A few years ago, I suffered from torsion of a testicle, and the Parole Board is making me feel the same way.

My tension eases as I focus on my relaxation techniques. Concentrate on the good thoughts, while breathing slowly. I visualize flies on my penis, the beach in summer, and a goat starving in Texas. This is starting to make me sleepy.

Mr. Barban thanks me for my time, and tells me they will be in touch. It's not like I had big plans for the day and they are holding me up. My greatest desire in life is to become a productive member of society. How can the Parole Board not love me?

Two days later, I receive the notice in my cell. My parole is approved, which allows me to remove the veil........

Someone is shaking me from a sound sleep, it's Mary.

Remembering my dream was not difficult, it was a recorded memory.

Tuesday

They say you can only feel one pain at a time, the worst pain will always override the lesser. This must be disappointing to the good folks who torture people. My tooth hurts, but my back doesn't. I grind my teeth constantly while sleeping, and it force's Mary to stick gum in my mouth. This allows her to rest in peace.

I need to make an appointment to see my dentist today. Dentists are not my favorite people, but I do admire their equipment.

The office answers on the first ring, and I'm impressed by their professionalism. The secretary has a soft voice, which induces me to masturbate as she asks me questions. She sets up an appointment for later in the afternoon.

Sex tends to make me drowsy, so after setting the

alarm, I flop down on the couch for a nap. Alarms are helpful, unless you are setting fires or escaping.

The aroma of burning trash hovers over the neighborhood. My fellow citizens burn their garbage in fifty gallon drums, rather than paying a garbage man. These drums can come in handy at times.

My brother learned to play drums at the age of twelve, shortly after his bout with meningitis. The disease infused Ralph with rhythm. These racing thoughts in my head, combined with the throbbing pain from my tooth, make it impossible to nap.

The buzzing alarm startles me from my reverie, and I quickly check outside to make sure the trees are where they should be. My mom used to cut down trees whenever she had the opportunity.

The tooth is mailing nerve pain to my brain, making me eager to get this taken care of. A corner broke off one of my lower right molars last night, and I must have swallowed it in my sleep.

My stool will need to be scrutinized for the next few days to see if it passes. During this process, pennies can be observed if you have consumed any. The coins are hard to locate unless they are new, but mom always told me any good effort would be rewarded.

My dentist's office is located in Ballston Spa, and I often wonder why he opened his business in such an odd village. It's a small country town where most of the residents are related. That's just another way of saying, everybody knows everybody.

The dentist's secretary looks nothing like I had imagined, there's no semen on her face, and she lacks traces of blood in her hair. If the opportunity arises, I will show her the washcloth in my pocket.

There are pictures of teeth plastered all over the walls of the waiting area, and it makes me want to bite somebody. I feel restless, but in a good way.

My dentist greets me from the hallway, and I follow him around the corner to one of the exam rooms. After sitting in the big boy chair, I look around the room for a bowl of porridge. There doesn't seem to be any cereal available, but there's a circular light shining down on my face. Should I smile?

Dr. Dryck is a short swarthy man, whose skin emits the odor of red onions. He begins his rapid examination of my mouth before there's opportunity to prepare. Nobody has ever seen what is behind my teeth.

The dentist could use a vowel in his name, and there are tiny little hairs on his fingers. Judging from my past experience, it's better to shave a peach before you eat it. If you can't trim it, at least comb it out once in a while. I contemplate biting off one of his fingers, but control the urge. Where's my razor when I need it?

Dr. Dryck informs me there's not enough tooth left to save, and he will need to extract it. I suggest he should return the tooth to me after it's pulled. From the expression on his face, you would think this is an unusual request. Over the years, I have learned not to leave parts of myself behind for others.

He injects two needles inside my mouth, and before long there's no feeling in my face or tongue. This is turning out to be enormous fun. I would love to drive an ice pick inside Dr. Dryck's ear. Unfortunately, I didn't bring one with me, and my lack of preparation is unsettling. The intense pain has caused me to overlook things.

Using massive effort, the dentist withdraws the tooth and packs the hole with gauze. It feels like a spider has crawled inside my mouth, but I manage to contain my scream. It proves that courage resides in all of us.

Apparently we are finished, and after sitting a few moments to make sure the bleeding has stopped, I'm allowed to leave. Did they really think anybody could stop me?

As I'm paying the receptionist, she hands me a plastic container with my tooth inside. My name is printed on the container, but it's spelled wrong, and this does not surprise me. There are no Nobel Laureates in the village.

She also gives me a prescription for vicodin, and that

brightens my day. Many good things start with the letter V. Vagina, virile, viper, vicious, vermin, vulva, and diazepam to name a few. I remove my tooth from the container, and wrap it inside the washcloth from my pocket.

After escaping from the dentist, I drive straight to the local pharmacy. Do I look suspicious? They fill my prescription, and I swallow three of the vicodin dry. You should never follow the instructions on the label, they are far too conservative.

By the time I arrive home, my tooth is still hurting. How can this be? The tooth is in my pocket. The hole where my tooth once lodged is what's causing the pain.

Having always been a quick thinker, I sprint to the shed behind my house. After acquiring the necessary tools, I hammer a nail through my foot.

The hole in my mouth does not hurt anymore.

Thursday

Money is paper. Sometimes, I worry about not having enough money, but I seldom worry about not having enough paper, unless parked on the toilet.

There's a hefty pile of bills stacked on top of the kitchen table, and it makes me wonder where they all came from. It seems like those bills were paid already, but it's hard enough to remember how the blood got on my shirt without having to think about which bills have been paid.

They usually send a return envelope with the bill, and it makes me feel like someone is trying to rush me. I have my own envelopes, and it's pleasurable to lick them.

My envelopes have no mind control medication mixed into the glue. This allows the natural flavor of granny smith apples to be savored by the licker. There are people trying to get inside my head, but there's no vacancy.

Writing checks to pay bills can be time consuming. My inner child hasn't grown fingers yet.

My checks have bounced at the bank from time to time. I try to make them bounce at home, but they just sit there, like Uncle Ed did when the brick landed on him. Bricks don't bounce far, but Uncle Ed recoiled off the floor a little. Red bricks are best, if you want to hide the blood.

Every other month, I pay my bills with money orders in order to change my patterns. There are assassins out there, and they are always watching me. I never drive the same route to work, or wear the same socks twice.

Paper comes from trees, and my checks are made of paper. My mom used to cut down trees, but she never had a paper cut. Some things in life are just not meant to be figured out.

Friday

Mary makes crafts from kits, and I am crafty. She likes putting things together, while I enjoy pulling things apart. Cartilage can be tough to separate from bone.

Mary's crafts come in small boxes through the mail, and I always want to rip them open, but she won't let me. Small boxes make me excited for some reason. That's the secret to a good marriage.

I step outside to check on the mail, and it looks like Mary has received another kit. Her kits come from the American Craft Company, but they are made in China which seems odd. The packages come once every month, and I wonder how they know the schedule. I come more than once a month, and that makes me extremely grateful.

Carrying the little cardboard box inside the house, I place it gently on the kitchen table. Lying there, it reminds me of my grandfather, who died on a kitchen table even though it wasn't in the kitchen.

Today is my day off, but Mary is at work, and I miss my wife terribly. Licking a butter paper from the garbage makes me feel a little better. I never lick margarine wrappers because it's bad for your heart.

Cars are driving by my house, and I have noticed they do this quite often. Every once in a while a police car will speed by, causing me to duck behind the couch. The police are not my friends, and when they knock on my door, I refuse to answer.

Grabbing the package from the table, I shake it vigorously, and it sounds like a baby's rattle. Snatching Scooter off the floor, I shake my cat and she yowls.

Comparing the two sounds to each other allows me to determine there's no cat inside the package. Scooter has run to the rear of the house to be alone. Small animals need to have private time. I enjoy solitude, but the voices always seem to follow me unless I'm in the shower. The water dilutes their power.

The doctor will give you remeron when he doesn't know what else to do.

Mary's previous kit was a bird house, and she completed it within one week. The door was too small for the birds to fit inside, so I poured a can of Slim Fast into their feeder. It's a husband's duty to be helpful.

Smelling the cardboard package makes me salivate, and I allow the slobber to drip from the corner of my mouth into Scooter's bowl. I spit on the floor at work, it expresses my disdain for the place. Mary does not allow me to do that at home.

Scooter has returned from her refuge, and is rubbing her soft head against my bare feet. I never realized my toes have fur on them. Scooter has fur all over her body, except for the spots where she got into the acid. I got into acid once, but it didn't burn.

Removing a butter knife from the silverware drawer, I scrape it across the package, and collect the debris in a zip lock bag. In life you have to take what you want, nobody is going to give you anything, unless you work for the government.

Before sealing the bag, I carry it down to the cellar, and smell the contents. It has an aroma similar to a cactus, but the package came from Cleveland, and the kits are from China. Is this a paradox? Sealing up the bag, I carefully place it on the shelf with the others, and wash my hands before returning upstairs.

My car is pulling into the driveway, and for a moment it makes me nervous, but then I notice it's just my wife. Where has she been all day? Life is such a mystery.

Greeting Mary at the door with a kiss, she smells like integrity. I encourage her to open the package on the table, and she concedes.

As she begins to rip off the sealing tape, it makes me wet my pants. Surprises very seldom turn out to be what you expect, but I remain hopeful.

Saturday

Upon arriving home, I begin to unpack the groceries from the car, but something is missing. Where's the cat litter? The bagger at the store was young, and more interested in talking to his friends than doing his job.

Did he put the litter in someone else's cart? I double check the trunk, no litter. There's a Necco Wafer on the wheel well, and I eat it. Nutrition is important to me.

Did the bagger leave the litter on the checkout counter? The incompetence makes me furious. Calling the store, they don't even give me a chance to talk before putting me on hold. There's no recorded music available, so I hum to myself. Mom always told me that I was adaptable, or was that adoptable.

Finally someone listens to my problem, puts me on hold for a second time, and goes to check with the bagger. When the customer service person returns to the phone, I am informed they questioned the young man, but he doesn't remember any cat litter. This is not the response I was looking for.

The friendly representative explains how the manager

will be happy to reimburse me, if I return to the store with a receipt. I slam down the phone. It's no longer about the cat litter, it's about the principle, and you have to pay interest first.

Scooter gazes up at me questioningly, and I yearn to squeeze her tail. While stroking her sway back, I apologize and attempt to explain about the missing litter. If the bagger had not packed my Fruit Loops it would have been acceptable, but my cat is innocent.

After obtaining my claw hammer from the basement, I get in the car and drive back to the supermarket. Looking through the window while parking, I can see my favorite employee is still working. Is this fate or karma? Who the fuck would work at a place named Piggly Wiggly anyway?

The bagger has red hair, and it will be a darker shade of that color soon. Both of my sisters had red hair, and that's why I'm glad they weren't around when I was growing up. They are half sisters, from my fathers first marriage, and were grown and on their own before I was born. My father is on his fifth marriage, the previous four wives are dead. One of my sisters is dead, which makes her easy to locate. The other sister is in California, and someday I will find her.

Red hair on humans is an aberration of nature. Baboons have a red ass, and so do Irishmen, proving that opposable thumbs do not necessarily make us better.

While waiting for the bagger to get off work, I wander the aisles of the store, and pick up a roll of duct tape. You can use duct tape to repair your car, or to fix life's problems. Justice is not that hard to come by, unless you live in Alabama.

When I rub my fingers along the vegetables in the produce section, the celery feels like the varicose veins in the backs of my legs.

I grab a box of garbage bags off the shelf, making sure they are the heavy duty brand. The box holds ten, which is probably more than I will need, but it's good to be prepared. This may be my opportunity to earn another merit badge.

Putting another bag of litter in my cart, I make sure its fresh scent. Scooter is sensitive about odors.

I open a bag of chocolate chip cookies, and begin munching on them while pushing the cart. Sometimes, I like to show off my coordination. Eating the cookies is not stealing, it's a way to momentarily satisfy my hunger. If a lion snaps off your arm and devours it, is that stealing? No, the lion is hungry.

My face is reflected back at me from the glass door of the freezer section. I look just like Richard Simmons without hair, and this depresses me, but not to the point of suicide. Tossing the rest of the cookies into the freezer, I make my way to the front of the store. My hunger has turned to other things.

Checking out at the same cashier as before, my eyes remain fixated on the young bagger. This time he puts the litter in my cart where it belongs. I forgive him for his earlier transgression, but I'm already out of the house, and the mission must be completed.

In the parking lot, I wait patiently in my car until I see the red headed fellow coming my way. I suddenly feel the urge to dance. The bagger's work is done, and now its hammer time.

My car is small, but it has a spacious trunk, and during the drive home the moans echoing from it mix well with the Jackie Wilson song playing on the radio. This was one of my favorite tunes, but today it sounds really special. It was probably digitally recorded.

Arriving home, I enter the house through the cellar door. Mary respects my privacy, and I respect my wife.

After taking the groceries upstairs, I start four large pots of meat boiling on the stove. It makes the kitchen smell just like Haiti. The meat makes its own gravy, and this should be enough to feed Scooter for several months.

Placing some of the meat in her bowl, I watch carefully as Scooter sniffs and samples. She likes it, but later she will have gas, it's not her usual brand.

I would like to taste the concoction myself, but most

pet food is not fit for human consumption. There's a large freezer in my cellar where I will store the excess meat.

For some reason this day has left me exhausted, so upon completion of this journal entry, it's off to bed for me.

Sunday

Sex is natural, like the potato chips in the red bag. My sexual experiences are limited to my wife, unless you count my hand, my pillow, a grapefruit, or my dad's tie. Some people are uncomfortable with sex, but I am miserable without it.

My first sexual experience with anyone other than myself was when I was twelve years old. I was not married at the time.

Mom and dad never paid much attention to me, unless I was shooting arrows at my brother. Ralph had some great reflexes in those days. My parents didn't teach me about the birds and bees, I was self instructed.

The house where we grew up had three bathrooms, two downstairs and one upstairs. The upstairs bathroom was exclusively mine after I smeared the walls with feces to mark my territory. Once it dried, the fragrance was similar to orange peels.

My mom wanted to clean it up, but dad told her to leave it alone. To this day, I'm not sure if he was talking about the walls or me. My father was a fun loving sociable character. He told mom, it was good to see me doing something constructive for a change.

In my private bathroom, I would half fill the tub with warm water, lay on my back, and arouse myself as the water rolled against my body. Then the exercise of catching the flies would begin. There were always great numbers of them in my bathroom for some unknown reason. The hard part was pulling off their wings without having casualties.

The wingless flies were carefully situated on the head

of my penis. They would scramble around in circles, with the water surrounding them. There was no escape. Sometimes, they would fall off, and rescues would need to be performed. The sensation of their little feet fluttering on my dick was exquisite. The more flies the merrier. They say your first sexual experience is the most memorable, and you will get no argument from me.

Now I'm married, and Mary does not know about the flies, or the grapefruit. Our marriage is built upon trust, not on shared information.

Marriage is a great institution, it enables you to access sex whenever you want it. It's not possible to rape your wife when it's her duty to meet your needs. How can a woman claim rape if she derived any pleasure from the act? Does hot wax leave scars?

Some people assert a woman always has the right to say no, but I disagree. The privilege to decline servicing your man is dissolved when the woman says, I do.

One night at dinner a few years ago, Mary wanted to know if I would like some gravy on my meat. My response was to decline. She suggested, I should at least try the gravy, but I firmly refused. My wife being her usual independent self, poured the gravy over my meat anyway. After tasting the dish, I discovered it was delicious.

Was I raped?

Monday

I have never liked people dropping by to visit without an invitation. Mary and Scooter are company enough for me. I am particular about who breaks bread with me.

Wilbert is a pleasant neighbor, but we have never shared a meal together. His cat will often wander onto my deck, despite the warning signs. Scooter doesn't like the neighbor's cat, and becomes agitated.

Today, the annoyance is greater than my patience. I

follow the neighbor's cat as it roams in the direction of my shed. Removing my baseball bat from the shed, I make sure my grip is secure.

The bat is wood not aluminum, and it resonates with the proper sound when you hit something. Wood is pure and natural, like masturbation.

Wilbert's kitty ambles right up to me, proving how animals can sense the kind-heartedness in people. When I swing the bat, it looks like a triple, but the kitty staggers to its feet. This makes me realize it was only a double.

Once more I swing with extra effort, and this time the crunch of the cat's spine echos across the yard. The sound of bones breaking arouses me, and makes me swing again, and again. I'm going to need a change of underwear, and I hope Mary did the laundry last night.

Wilbert is standing on his porch watching me, and it has always been my desire to remain friendly with my neighbors. I wave to him with the hand not holding the bat. He runs inside his house, and slams the door shut. A few years ago, he called the police to come and offer me assistance, but he has learned not to repeat that behavior. Who says you can't teach an old dog new tricks.

I wipe my bloody bat off on the lawn, and place it tenderly back inside the shed. The mixtures of colors smeared on the grass remind me of Christmas, and a wave of joy rolls over me.

There is always a baseball bat close by, but the game itself does not interest me. During my youth, my dear father tied me to a tree, and threw baseballs at me. He mentioned something about a learning curve.

It looks like Wilbert's cat has passed away beside my shed, and the neighborly thing would be to let him know. First things first.

Going inside, I wrap Scooter up in my arms, and carry her outside to see the dead kitty. Scooter sniffs her old friend one time and runs back toward the house. She can't stay outside long because she has been declawed. This makes her a house cat, and also means she doesn't scratch me when I'm naked.

A few years ago, I peeled all the nails off my toes. My feet hurt for a long time after that. The nails had turned a sickly yellow color.

Yellow is not a bad color, but it associates with awful things, such as yellow streak, yellow fever and the dreaded mellow yellow. Wilbert's dead kitty is yellow.

As I walk next door, my plan is to give Wilbert the bad news. When I knock, there's no answer. He is probably taking a nap.

I gently place the yellow cat on his doorstep, just as any responsible citizen would do. I briefly consider leaving a note, but it would be redundant. This is self explanatory.

As I walk back home, the lessons taken from this day settle into my soul.

Tuesday

On the drive to work, I notice that D V Loves Norma was painted on the train overpass during the night. Why would D V want his personal message out in the open where everybody can see it? What about the privacy of the individual? Apparently, D V has not heard about Hippa.

Taking my cell phone from between my legs, I call out sick in order to investigate this mystery. I'm never really sick, but it's an acceptable excuse when you want a day off.

Sometimes my stomach gets upset, causing me to vomit, but barfing doesn't qualify as sickness. If you notice mucous in your vomit, it should be saved and examined. You should never under any circumstances vomit on your car, your foot, or your wife. Dogs like to gobble up vomit, but there is never one around when you need them.

Pulling over onto the shoulder of the road, I park and begin to plan my ascent to the overpass. There seems to be a clear path between the pine trees on the left side of the high-way. After locking the car, I begin the challenging ascension.

I always lock my car to protect the personal items, like the cereal bowl under my seat.

By the time I reach the summit of the hill, my breathing is ragged. It made me wish for a cigarette, even though I don't smoke. Butting a cigarette out on the top surface of my foot helps me concentrate. This is a well known medical technique called reflexology, and it enables me to maintain my excellent reflexes.

I have reached my destination, in spite of my shortness of breath. Before proceeding onto the overpass, I need to make sure the tracks are clear. Safety was ingrained into me by my mom at an early age. You can't be too careful around chainsaws.

While the tracks remain clear, I place my ear to the rail and listen. It sounds like my brother is calling me. Ralph and I lived in a mobile home when we were growing up. The home did not move much, but we did. The Christmas fire put an end to my father's dreams of affordable housing.

There were train tracks running through our back yard, and the steam engines clattered when they went speeding by at night. The vibrations rippling through the ground caused the trailer to shake as bad as Ralph, after he caught meningitis.

It was entertaining to put quarters on the tracks, so the trains could run over them during the night. After a train passed by, I would grab a flashlight, and run outside to retrieve them. Some of the coins would be smashed flat, but others vanished into thin air. Carrying the flattened quarters inside the trailer, I would wake up my brother and make him smell them. Ralph learned to distinguish many kinds of scents, but his nose would bleed.

One night, I convinced Ralph to join me on coin retrieval, even though he had declined previously. When the train was almost on top of us, I gave my brother a little shove in the back, just for fun. Ralph was an agile child, and the train missed. I miss my brother, but there's a railroad spike in my car trunk to remind me of him.

After the train incident, our parents sent me away to

live on a farm for six months. Ralph was allowed to remain at home, he was the favorite child.

Farms can be amusing, once you get used to the atmosphere. There were no trains on the farm, but they did have one red tractor with huge tires. There were several violent incidents involving the tractor and other residents during my stay.

There were also horses on the farm, and it always felt like they were watching me. When a horse stares at you, the world is no longer safe.

Standing in the center of the overpass, I can see for miles in all directions. There's no reason for me to believe anyone is returning my gaze.

A sponge can only retain so much water before it begins leaking. The overpass is a spiritual place, and it overwhelms me to the point of tears.

The affectionate words that D V painted on the overpass are in fluorescent orange. It appears to be reflective paint, and I am a reflective human being.

There are cars full of people passing beneath me, and it makes me curious about where they are going. The voice within explains, they are losers on their way to work.

After stumbling back down the hill, I thoroughly examine the bush growing next to my car before unlocking the door. Sometimes you can find things in bushes, but not this one.

If the people of this country had checked the bush before unlocking the door, we would not be in the situation we are today.

Wednesday

My garbage man comes once a week on Wednesday, and I come whenever the opportunity arises. The trash man charges me four dollars for each bag he picks up. At my house, there's one bag waiting every week. A big one.

In the country, a lot of people burn their garbage in big metal drums. I enjoy burning things, but not garbage. The trash can't whimper.

My garbage man is old and short, while I'm old and tall. His name is Pete, my name is Lyam. Both of our names have four letters, and he charges me four dollars every week. This is a world where coincidences worry me, and make me apprehensive.

It takes a long time for Pete to climb in and out of his truck, due to the fact his legs are very short. He has a small head with oversized ears, like a Hobbit. When he retires, I would like to hang his head on my bedroom wall, but Mary will have to be informed ahead of time. My wife does not like surprises, unless they are green.

As Pete tosses my single bag into his truck, I decide to follow him, and see where he goes with my garbage. After all, it's a part of me.

It doesn't take me long to catch up with the garbage truck, as Pete continues his pick ups. Most of his stops have two bags waiting at the curb, but this doesn't seem to annoy him.

I am the proud owner of two testicles, but they came with only one bag. I wonder if anyone has been born with three testicles. There was a woman who lived in the center of Corinth, and she had three teeth, but nobody took any.

Some of the garbage bags have ties around the top, and others do not. I will never wear a tie, but they do come in handy for other purposes. Following Pete is turning out to be an educational experience.

A few of the bags he picks up are clear, but most are solid black. I always prefer to use black bags, the clear ones can be too revealing. My wife thinks, I'm overly protective of my neighbors.

Pete has never revealed his last name to me, and I have never asked what his hands smell like. The information highway ends at my house.

He parks at Town Hall for a pickup, and there are close to twenty bags stacked next to the dumpster. I cruise through the intersection and pull over, in case this takes a while.

In the corner of my mind, there's an unpleasant memory surfacing. It involved my bodily removal from Town Hall shortly after we first moved to this quaint village. It was during an open school budget meeting, when the town wanted to waste a ton of money on a new school and buses.

They were receiving comments and suggestions from the taxpayers. I waited patiently until my chance finally came, and then questioned the good townspeople about why we needed a new school, when most of the children in town are retarded.

It's prudent to avoid bringing problems to light without also offering a solution. I suggested, the children would be better served if they were sent to the vocational school in Saratoga. This would alleviate the need for a new school, and render tax relief to the local citizens. The vocational school has its own blue buses.

My little speech caused quite a stir, proving once again how country people have no control over their emotions. They bodily removed me from the building, and I have never returned to the Town Hall until now. I raise my middle finger to the building, but it's not an act of anger. I don't feel anything inside. It's like putting Orajel on ants, they can't feel their legs.

Pete has moved further down the road, so I cease my reminiscing and continue to follow him. He makes a right turn, and we have arrived at the town dump. The dump is only a short distance from Town Hall, and this detail does not escape me. The odor emanating from the dump smells like sausage that's been out in the sun for too long.

Pete has started unloading his truck by hand. He's a hard worker, and I'm extremely proud of my garbage man. Beeping my horn nearly makes him jump out of his skin. Another fact about country folk is they are pretty easy to scare.

In spite of his nervousness, Pete smiles and waves in my direction. This is a good thing. I have a low tolerance for rude people.

I exit the dump, and quickly drive back home. Along the way, I write down the addresses of the people who left out more than two bags of garbage.

Next week, Pete should not have to work so hard.

Thursday

When there's nothing else to do, I will look through the phone directory. It always amazes me how many names are listed. I managed to memorize seven pages once, but it brought on a headache, and caused the voices to wake up.

With a good imagination you can put faces to the names, and other body parts. Looking at the names, makes me feel like I'm part of the big picture.

My doctor believes I have a personality disorder, but that is unacceptable. The medications he prescribed make people stare at me.

I have stopped taking all the medications, except for the ginkgo biloba. The biloba will allow me to think clearly, and it's gentle on my stomach.

You should never randomly call people, because they may have caller ID. I prefer not to draw any extra attention to myself. Otherwise, you are forced to turn problems into solutions.

If the print in the directory was larger, the numbers would be easier to read. There are times in life, when I wish other things were bigger. The eyes are not always the first organs to go.

To avoid the danger from jaundice, you should never touch the yellow pages. There are numerous diseases in the world, and quite a few of them begin with the word yellow. Always wear latex gloves, as a precautionary measure.

The color yellow by itself is not harmful, in fact I love to eat yellow chicks during the Easter holiday. The other colors have never appealed to me, but this doesn't make me a racist.

There's a stack of phone books in the corner of my kitchen, and a mound of femur bones in my cellar. I am not a chiropractor. The bones never remain stacked as neatly as the books.

Every year, somebody places a new phone book on the ground beside my mailbox. Most of the names inside are the same, but there are always a few additions, and it makes me wonder why they weren't in the previous book. Were they trying to hide something? With a blue magic marker, I highlight the new names.

My name is not in the phone book. I have an unlisted number, but it doesn't protect me from receiving calls from friendly people attempting to sell me something. They talk rapidly, as if trying to confuse me, and it requires two valium for me to understand.

Mary constantly reminds me to throw out the old phone books, but I refuse. She treats me like a child, and there's a day of reckoning coming.

During my childhood, there were days when mom and dad went off to work, leaving me to take care of my brother. One day, right after they left the house, I glued my brother's hand to the toilet seat. Ralph stayed there for the whole day, until mom came home from work. My brother was extremely hungry, but not thirsty.

He should have had a phone book.

Friday

When I was a little kid, dog biscuits were one of my favorite snacks. I can't remember the brand, but they were better than mom's cookies, and more accessible.

Dogs will lick you until you can't stand it anymore, and they never ask for much in return. After Speedy died, my dad got us another dog named Frisky. He was a Boston bull dog, with big bulging eyes that watered when I pinched his legs. Frisky's breath smelled unusually sweet, and I assumed he was a diabetic. We never had him tested, but the suggestion was offered.

My wife is a diabetic, and while she was sleeping, I licked her eye. It was sweeter than expected. The eyes are the mirrors to our souls, but Mary's eye did not taste like our mirror.

Just for kicks one day, I sampled one of Scooter's cat treats, but they were not as flavorful as dog biscuits.

This morning, I had to phone the veterinarian to ask how much it would cost to cut off a cat's tail. Scooter has a large growth on the base of her tail, and it's starting to smell. The vet suggested, the cat needed to be examined before any decision was made concerning amputation. He transferred me to his receptionist, and she gave me an appointment to bring Scooter in this afternoon.

My kitty pretended to lack interest when I explained about going to visit the doctor. She hates traveling to the vet, and expresses this animosity by vomiting inside the car. I brought a coffee can, to scoop up the vomit. It's a Maxwell House can, and it's good to the last drop. Scooter does not disappoint me.

After arriving at the veterinarian's office, I stagger slightly when getting out of the car. This causes Scooter to clasp onto my neck desperately, and once again, I'm grateful she's been declawed. I make a mental note to have my tires aligned because my balance seems to be off.

The vet's new Mazda is parked right beside my car, enabling me to deposit the dripping coffee can on his back seat. This is one more example of why you should always lock your vehicle. The best gifts are the ones we don't expect. His car smells like ganja, and it makes me curious about what he eats for breakfast.

Carrying my kitty into the office, I sign in with the receptionist. Scooter has never learned how to write. I take a seat in the waiting room, and hold her in my lap. She's trembling slightly, and I'm hoping she won't wet herself. I tighten my grip around her body. A man and his kitty have a unique bond.

Scooter makes unusual noises when she's anxious, and the folks in the office are looking in our direction. People are always watching me, but Scooter is shy. I encircle my fingers gently around her throat, and she quickly settles down.

The vet is inviting us into one of the rooms on the left side of the hallway. I remember this room from the last time we were here, it's the same room where Scooter was diagnosed with worms. This time, he places my cat on a steel table in the center of the room. Where the fuck is the Jamaican hiding?

The steel table seems to be missing something, but I can't put my finger on it. Suddenly, I realize the missing component is a sharp instrument, and it's difficult to hide my disappointment.

The vet pokes and prods at Scooter until she tries to bite him. She's a good kitty. Taking off my belt, I put it in my pocket, to be prepared like Betty Crocker.

The vet gives Scooter a shot for rabies, and this catches me off guard, I didn't realize she was rabid. Scooter bit me a few days ago, and I question him about a shot for myself, but the vet looks at me like I'm crazy. Where have I seen that look before?

He explains how the lump on Scooter's tail is not serious, and at this juncture should be left alone. I request to see his license, and he starts to perspire profusely. Never under any circumstances trust sweaty people, under the coating of sweat they are hiding something.

Scooping Scooter into my arms, we escape from the exam room, I pay the receptionist and leave. You should never waste your time in a place where you are not welcome.

In the parking lot, Scooter commands me to release the air from the vet's tires. She may not be able to write, but she is able to whisper instructions. My cat has a very soft voice, so it's important to tell the other voices in my head to shut up. Letting the air out of the tires alleviates the pain behind my left ear.

Scooter reciprocates by not vomiting on the ride home.

Later that evening, I slipped my kitty a sedative, and cut the lump off her tail myself. The tumor was a solid chunk of tissue, not liquid like I thought it would be. I placed the moist lump in a clean mason jar and put it in the cupboard.

Mary will assume it's garlic, and it should add a nice kick to a sauce.

Saturday

It involved badgers in 1974, coy dogs in 1988, and the people from town in 2000. Now in 2006, its squirrels. I first noticed them gathering around my house at breakfast time. It is my normal routine to skip breakfast, but I drink a tall glass of cranberry juice every morning. It makes my urine shine.

Looking inside my first aid kit, it seems to be in good order. There's a full box of band aids, one roll of gauze, a pair of scissors, and one condom. Preparation is everything in life.

The squirrels have completely surrounded my home. There's one squirrel in the front yard, nine in the back yard, five on the left side of the house, and I count two on the right side. 1-9-5-2. How did the squirrels figure out I was born in 1952? Thankfully, no squirrels are on the roof, which means I will not die this year.

The squirrels don't seem to be maneuvering into at-tack positions, but they continue to watch my house in the same manner that I scrutinize my neighbor's. I admire their strict discipline.

Removing one bag of Scooter's fur from the closet, I burn a small tuft in the kitchen sink. The fur had some dander in it, and I struggle to avoid sneezing. I can't afford to make any noise, or the squirrels will determine my location. They have an acute sense of hearing.

Sticking one finger into the ashes, I draw a semicolon on my chest. This will warn the squirrels about my affiliation with wildlife organizations. The squirrels have not moved from their positions, and I wonder if they are domesticated.

Scooter wants to know what's going on, and she squirms with interest as I hold her up to the window. When I press her labia against the screen, three of the squirrels wink at her. Putting my kitty back on the floor, she scampers rapidly down the hall. She will not be seen again for three days, the allotted time for cleansing.

Using my binoculars, I try to determine how many nipples each of the squirrels have. Having three of my own, I imagine they have more. The observation angles are all wrong, not allowing me to get an accurate count. Do squirrels breast feed? If I poisoned their milk would it be considered biological warfare? What does squirrel milk taste like? This business is starting to make me thirsty.

Mary is pulling into the driveway from work, and the squirrels continue to encircle the house. I'm afraid for her, yet at the same time tingling with anticipation to see if the animals will attack.

My wife makes it safely inside, and I seek her advice on how to handle the squirrel problem. She laughs at me, which makes me consider holding her labia up to the window, but I don't have an ergometer in the house. People have laughed at me all my life, and I have most of their teeth in my cellar.

Removing my shoes and socks, I prepare to go outside and do battle. The squirrels have suddenly become agitated, so I slide the ocean sound's CD into the player, and crank it up to maximum volume. The animals are calming down, but Mary appears to be getting upset.

While making her some tea, I add one xanax, stirring briskly to make sure it's completely dissolved. She drinks the tea and settles down. I love my wife, but she should be grateful that she married a nurturing man.

Proceeding outdoors, I'm careful not to make eye contact with the squirrels. You should never try to dominate wild animals or a short lesbian.

There's a piece of litmus paper in my pocket, in case the opportunity arises to obtain some urine from the animals. The squirrels have shown little interest in my movements, but I remain alert.

Removing the gas can from my shed, I rub my arms and neck with a thin layer of fuel. You need to be safety conscious while doing this, but the gasoline keeps the mosquitos away. If the squirrels manage to overrun my position, the matches are a last resort.

After putting the can back inside the shed, I pull out the lawnmower. It starts easily, and to my great surprise most of the squirrels have started to run away. I chase the remainder of them with the mower, but they all escape. Some folks were not as lucky when I used the shotgun in 2000.

Mary is standing in the doorway, calling me to come inside for supper, but her voice seems slurred. The medication should allow me to take advantage of her, and I won't be required to wear a condom.

I secure the perimeter, and go inside the house. During supper my attention is fixed on the yard, I know the squirrels will be coming back. Mary wants to know why my feet are green.

Sunday

Sometimes it's relaxing to just get in your car and drive with no destination in mind. If you are able to avoid distractions, there are many things you can do while driving a car. Most of them are legal.

When the double yellow lines in the center of the road change to a single line, I pull over to the side and urinate. Most of the time, I will step outside the car, but on rainy days I remain inside the vehicle and use an Arizona Tea bottle. They are the ones with the large opening.

The voices inside my head have been mumbling lately, making it difficult to obtain directions. I follow the silver Ford in front of me. How in the world do the birds ever find their way south?

I prefer my eggs scrambled, and birds lay eggs, but they won't eat them. They don't eat candy either, but ants do, and insects will devour the birds if they fall on the ground. My ability to reason things out, grants me understanding.

There's a yield sign at the next corner, and I wonder what would happen if I refuse to yield. Would this act of rebellion on my part cause an earthquake?

We lived in California for a few years when I was a child, and earthquakes happened quite often. A real good one could rattle your testicles and make you happy.

Our front yard in Pasadena was dark green ivy instead of grass, and it turned into a natural habitat for lizards. I liked to feed the reptiles to our stupid bulldog. Frisky got sick, and the lizards died.

After thirty minutes of following the silver Ford, my sense of direction returns, allowing me to head back home. A car speeds by in the opposite lane, and a dog is hanging its head out the rear window. The dog looks so happy, it makes me wonder what medications it's on.

If only there were a way for me to hang my penis out the window.

Wednesday

The Fourth of July will be here in a few days, signaling the beginning of the end for summer. Summer is my favorite season of the year, the sun radiates on my skin, and makes me horny.

Barbecues are the choice events during summer, fire and flesh are a perfect combination. Only charcoal can cook meat properly, that's why you will never see a gas grill on my deck.

Hot coals and tongs also work well together if you are careful. At night you can toss the embers at neighbors, and make your own fireworks.

I enjoy my steaks rare, while Mary prefers her meat well done. We are opposites in many ways. She does not have a penis, but I do, and over the years this has worked out well for us.

At some point during my youth, I acquired a taste for blood. It drives me to stir the crimson juice from rare steaks into my mashed potatoes.

Several years ago, I infused some leftover blood from the cellar into the toothpaste. My idea was to market it as a new brand called Plasmadent. Mary had no knowledge of the experiment. A husband should never tell his wife everything, unless he desires to die violently.

Blood tastes like a morning sunrise. By the age of eight, I had already learned how to suck on pennies, in order to savor the coppery flavor.

Mary's in the kitchen preparing the steaks, while I remain on the deck, guarding the fire. For a moment, it looks like mom's face in the flames, but she didn't have a mole on her chin.

Yesterday, my dentist extracted a tooth, and it requires me to chew on the right side of my mouth. In life you either learn to adapt or you die.

Where once there was a left lower molar, now there's an empty hole. I like holes, especially when allowed to fill them, but the hole in my mouth makes me feel vacuous.

Going inside to use the bathroom, I purposely splatter some piss on the tile, it sounds like a clown laughing. Looking in the mirror, I open my mouth and examine the crater.

The gum surrounding the hole undulates, and attempts to speak. It lacks teeth, and I can't understand a fucking thing it's saying. I listen intently for thunder, but don't hear any.

After rinsing out my mouth with salt water, I look in

the mirror again, and the hole appears to be laughing at me. This makes me want to scream, but I can't. Mary will hear me, and she doesn't permit me to make noise in the bathroom. My wife brings structure to my life.

The hole could be a bad influence on my other teeth, and this concerns me. Rebellion is a serious issue, which compels me to take some type of action. My other teeth don't shift, as they wait for my next move. You gain everybody's attention when you are unpredictable.

Running to the kitchen, I scoop a gob of peanut butter with my finger and return to the bathroom. Mary makes no attempt follow me, so it's not necessary to hide my tracks.

Using the mirror to guide my hand, I pack the hole in my mouth with the peanut butter. The result makes the hole look just like Scooter's ass. This was an unexpected outcome. I poke around the edge of the hole with a creosote toothpick, until it begins to bleed. This is making me hungry.

When I return to the kitchen, Mary has finished rubbing the steaks with spices. I take them outside, and toss them on the hot grill, inhaling the fragrance of raw flesh cooking as the meats sizzle.

I love to scratch my nails over the top of flesh, but not my own. The sensation of a sharp razor on my belly can be pleasant. Last year, I shaved all the fur from Scooter's front legs. She didn't want to hold still, and had to be restrained. Animals don't realize you are trying to help them, and people can be the same way.

Flipping the steaks over, I scrape my fingernails along the surface of the meat, and shout out to Mary that the food is ready. While waiting for her arrival, I noisily suck the bloody juice from beneath my nails. The flavor is intense.

Thursday

There are twenty trees bordering my property where the grass ends in the back yard. While surveying the perimeter of my land, I reiterate my oath to protect those trees with my life. Walking barefoot in the grass, makes my toe's tickle, and it stimulates me to chuckle. It's a hollow sound. The grass is dark green, and my feet are a pale disgusting white. The trees seem to enjoy the contrast.

As I reach the edge of my property, a wild desire erupts in my heart, to climb one of the trees towering over my head. Fortunately, I understand this would not be prudent at my age.

At the age of eight, I discovered the wondrous joy of climbing trees. Many remarkable things happened in my eighth year of life, and my body still bears the scars from some of them. My flesh was my father's tapestry.

You can tell the age of a tree, by counting the rings in its trunk after you cut it down. It's not accurate with people, but it took me several tries before I understood that point.

My mom was an angry bitter woman, and she expressed her anger by cutting down trees. I prefer chopping down people, but never in anger, emotions detract from the pleasure of the act. Anger never solves anything, but action does. Most people consider me a jovial man.

I can still remember how beautiful the views were from the top of a tree, and how the rough bark bit into my bare legs. Wearing shorts is a prerequisite for climbing. While sitting on a branch, I would furiously swing my legs back and forth, until my thighs would bleed. Mom used cocoa butter on the wounds to eliminate excessive scarring.

It was entertaining to carry objects up the tree and drop them. Balls bounce, but my brother didn't. Actually, Ralph did bounce a little bit, but I think the ground was too soft to get the desired results.

My brother is four years younger than I, and quite a bit shorter. He has one twisted leg from an accidental fall. The hospital helped him recover, but it didn't do much for me.

It was after Ralph's terrible tumble, that mom began cutting down the trees, but the good thing about trees is, you can always find more unless you live in Brazil.

Trees are like balloons at a carnival, or priests at the train platform, they are always there.

The Fourth of July is coming soon, and the town will be having fireworks at the fairgrounds. If you soak a cat in gasoline and carry it to the top of a tree, they don't seem to mind. When you light the cat, and toss it from the tree it makes fireworks. It should be performed at dusk, for the best visual effects. It's similar to a screaming bottle rocket, but cheaper.

I always wanted to attempt it with people, but they were far too heavy for me. My brother was a lightweight.

In order to protect my heart, I take one aspirin every day. Aspirin comes from the willow tree, and it makes me wonder if my pills came from one of the trees mom cut down.

Saturday

If you stick a straw in a dog's ear don't go around it with a milkshake. My father taught me lots of things when I was growing up, and it gives me good reason to despise him even today.

I can remember the first time my dad took me fishing when I was nine years old. We had to leave for the lake early in the morning, and dad reminded me over and over not to forget the beer. Ralph was only five years old, and he stayed home because he was afraid of the water.

It was a two-hour ride north to Indian Lake, and during the drive dad never spoke, but he watched me out of the corner of his eye. We never saw any Indian's at the lake, but when I mentioned it, dad called me an asshole, and told me to shut up and fish. He could speak one word, and make you want to run away.

He called me a sissy when I couldn't put a worm on the hook, but now I realize he was only trying to instruct me. My dad was a patient man, always willing to teach me things. He offered to show me the back of his hand more times than I can count.

Fishing can be boring, and my thoughts would drift away to safer places. That day, I reminisced about my dog Speedy, and how he met his maker. Lessons were learned that day, without getting my knuckles cracked.

I was seven years old, patiently waiting for the school bus, when I spotted Speedy lying in the middle of the road. He had been struck by a vehicle, and my first thought was to run back to the house, and alert my dad. My dad was a curious man, and he demanded to know what the hell I did to the dog.

Together we strolled to the edge of the road, and his grip on my shoulder eased enough to enable me to point at the smear of Speedy. My father was decisive, instructing me not to move while he went for a shovel. While he was on his recovery mission, I massaged my shoulder.

Dad's expression was grim as he returned with the spade, and I just knew we were going to have one of those precious father and son moments that you never forget.

He explained, how everybody ends up dead, and told me to get used to it. Over the years, I not only got used to death, but I acquired a taste for it. Dad handed me the shovel, and told me to scrape up Speedy, but I couldn't bring myself to do it. I started crying like a baby. That dog was one of the few living things who loved me.

My father called me a pussy, and at the time, I didn't have a clue what he was talking about. Now, I know exactly what pussy is, and I love it, but would still prefer not to be one. Dad clipped me in the head with the shovel handle, and scooped up Speedy in one smooth motion. My father may have been one of the first multi-taskers. Lying in the shovel, Speedy looked just like Aunt Amy after her stroke, except my aunt drooled more.

In the backyard, dad called me a worthless shit, and told me to dig the grave. He never wanted me to think too highly of myself. He was stern, but fair. After digging a shallow hole, my father scraped Speedy off the shovel with his boot, and together we pushed the dirt on top. I had seen my father bury things before, but this was the first time he let me help. The soil smelled like my father's hands.

Dad said a quick prayer, being a man of few words. Memories of the past, can be a comfort to a tortured mind, but you need to come back to reality or you will be lost.

At Indian Lake, we still hadn't seen any Indian's. After sitting on a log for an hour, dad was almost out of beer, and had a strange troubled look in his eye.

Suddenly, he got a bite on his line, and reeled in a good sized fish. He instructed me to remove it from the hook, but the fish slipped out of my hands, and damn near flopped back into the lake. Dad managed to grab the fish, glare at me simultaneously and mumble something about throwing me into the water. His statement confused me because I was already baptized.

My father was a wise man, who never received the credit he deserved. He began to gut the fish with a knife from his boot, and years later I would shit in the same boot, and learn to use knives. Every experience acquired in this lifetime is a debt owed to my father.

After removing the guts, he yanked up some grass and stuffed it inside the fish. When I questioned the purpose of using the grass, he told me it was to keep the fish fresh, and added I was an asshole for asking. My father did not like being interrogated.

When he wasn't looking, I scooped up the fish guts and stuffed them inside my sock.

I caught nothing that day, and on the ride home neither of us spoke, which was not a bad thing. A boy and his dad don't need words to express their love for each other.

At home, mom fried the fish for dad, while I took my sock filled with guts and hid it under his pillow.

Later that night, my father came into my room with an extension cord in his hand.

Monday

Crying is like washing organic laundry, and today I'm running a double load. Tears are streaming down my face, causing the road to blur as I drive to work. This has been happening ever since I stopped taking the medications. Should I pull off the road and cut myself? Sometimes cutting relieves the pressure, but usually it just makes a mess on the upholstery.

Snot is flowing from my nose, and I wonder if it could be opiate withdrawal. Parking along the shoulder of the road, I finish off the blunt left over from breakfast. There's just enough to settle my nerves, and keep me from shaking. You have to take control of your life through self medication.

After blowing my nose, I suck the rest of the snot from the back of my throat into my mouth. Sometimes you can get a chunk to chew on, but this isn't my lucky day.

With my excretions under control, I need to get my bearings and be back on the way to work. I don't need my map, the path to my job is well traveled. There are three very important items inside my glove compartment, a knife, a map, and a zip lock bag. There are no gloves in the box, thanks to what happened to O. J.

I push in the cigarette lighter, and after a moment it pops back out like magic. There's a telephone pole next to my car, and I concentrate on it while pressing the lighter into my calf until the flesh starts to smoke like Uncle Percy. My outlook on life is beginning to improve.

Another crop circle has appeared on my leg, but there are no clues how it got there. Should I call CNN to investigate? My leg could be an advertisement for the next Olympic games.

Getting out of the car, I stand beside the pole, close enough to smell the creosote. It's a good clean odor, like curdled blood on fresh snow.

Wires run from the pole beside me, to other poles

down the length of the road. It makes me feel connected to the world. Pacing off the distance to the next pole while snapping my fingers, I count forty-six steps. This is kind of interesting, but not enough to command my attention.

I walk back to the car, not snapping my fingers, but rubbing myself instead. We always get back to our basic animal needs.

Driving forward to the next pole takes me eight seconds without speeding. Standing next to the second pole, the wild desire to climb begins building up inside me. There's no other traffic on the road this morning, which gives me the courage to scamper partway up.

I consider climbing back down, but I'm wearing my lucky blue shirt, and the good fortune drives me higher. A cackling crow lands on the wire over my head, and I wait patiently to see if somebody flips the fry switch. To my great disappointment the execution is delayed. Having satisfied my adventurous spirit, I begin the climb down.

A car parks behind mine, a man exits the vehicle, and shades his eyes to look up at me. People just won't leave me alone in spite of the warning stickers behind my corneas.

The curious man wants to know if he can be of assistance. I ask if he has a claw hammer while rapidly climbing down to greet him. The good Samaritan jumps inside his car and drives off with tires squealing. There was a time when people were a lot more friendly.

Kissing the telephone pole goodbye, I let my tongue slip into the rough crevices until the intoxicating flavor fills my soul.

It looks like I'm going to be late for work again.

Tuesday

From Scooter's reaction it's safe to assume that cat's don't like washing machines. There's no survey data available for me to study.

Mary likes washing machines because you can get a good rhythm going if the washer is the right height. A short washer works best, so you don't injure your back. It takes a little effort to put salt in a giraffe's eye.

While short washers are wonderful, short people can be a pain in the ass. It's impossible to see them unless you are looking down all the time, and this causes people to think you lack confidence.

My greatest joy in life is to be of service to my fellow man whenever possible. A few years ago, I attempted to stretch a short person in my cellar, but they become unhinged much too early in the process. They also make a horrendous amount of noise even when you ask them nicely to be quiet.

Before Mary left for work this morning, she informed me the washer was making strange noises. When my wife gives me information, she expects me to act on it. Most of the time, I prefer strange noises, but my wife is not always comfortable with them.

I have never claimed to be mechanically inclined, but I'm willing to look inside the washer anyway. The tumbler spins smoothly and everything seems to be in working order.

I brought some tools up from the cellar in order to be prepared for any eventuality. When I tap the washer's side with my claw hammer, the booming sound resonates inside my head. If my brother was here, I could make him dance to the beat.

Claw hammers are one of my favorite multi purpose tools, but it takes practice to peel off the skin with the claw after you stun something. They are also handy if you need to scoop out eyes. A soup spoon will work just as well, or you can use your thumb to give a personal touch to your work. If the person has a glass eye, you must exercise extreme care not to break it. Seven years of bad luck is something nobody needs.

I decide to wash a load of dirty clothes, in order to hear the noise my wife described. The washer starts without any problem, but the only noise discernable is a faint humming in my head which is more comforting than strange.

There's an indentation on the left side of the washer's outer skin, where the machine was hit with a crossbow bolt several years ago. Scooter's litter box sits on the floor beside the washer, and the dent is about four inches above the box. Cats are agile animals.

Claw hammers are also great for dislocating bones, but you have to get your torque just right. If the claw is sharp, it can be used to lift up fingernails, but it's not sanitary to use it on toenails. Whoever invented the claw hammer was a genius.

The machine goes through the wash cycle without any problems, spin and rinse are next. It completes the rinse process and begins to spin out. The unusual noise that Mary found so disturbing is apparently gone.

There's a heavy thumping sound vibrating inside my head as if someone were trying to escape from a cellar. It's not coming from the washer, but I'm unable to determine the rackets origin.

The wash is completed, and after hanging up the clothes to dry, I write out a detailed bill for Mary. We do not own a dryer for safety reasons.

The washing machine is silent, but the rhythmic pounding continues inside my head. The relief I need can be found in the cellar.

The claw hammer comes with me in case adjustments are necessary. My hands are squeaky clean.

Wednesday

After a difficult day at work, I'm relaxing at home while watching the news. The sunglasses remain on my face so the television reporter will not notice me staring. I respect his privacy and expect the same in return.

Prairie dogs seem to be the headline news this evening. They appear kind of cute, and it makes me want to squeeze one until its eye's pop out.

The gist of the story is that prairie dogs are somehow infecting people with monkey pox. Apparently the monkey pox originated in a rat, and then infected the prairie dogs, who have now passed it off to humans. This is like a bizarre hot potato game.

The disease is similar to chickenpox, and is preventable by taking the smallpox vaccine. There don't seem to be any monkeys involved in the story, making me wonder why they are calling it monkey pox. The story does not make any damn sense.

The pictures of people infected with the monkey pox are quite intriguing. Their bodies are covered with oozing blisters that the reporter claims will eventually dry up and scab over. This shit is better than watching a scary movie.

The reporter is holding a prairie dog, and the tiny animal resembles Geraldo Rivera. The animal appears trapped and frightened, like my brother did after I tied him to a truck tire and rolled it down a hill.

Ralph screamed, but we were out near the edge of the woods and nobody heard him. He was still yelling as the tire collided with a tree at the bottom of the hill. It was one of the few trees mom failed to cut down.

Ralph's defective character caused him to run home before we could roll the tire again. He could still run pretty fast even though he had a bum leg.

The reporter is explaining how monkey pox may turn out to be an epidemic. I caught chickenpox at the age of thirty and it damn near killed me. The disease left me sterile, but I still wear a glove just in case. They can be used five times if you tie off each finger after filling.

Mary has joined me on the couch to watch the end of the news. We seem to be doing a lot of things together lately, but I still masturbate in between sessions.

I offer to check her for monkey pox, but she declines, and it makes me suspicious. After she falls asleep, I will perform a secret inspection.

After the news is over, maybe I will call the local pet store to see if they have any prairie dogs available.

Thursday

How can you be sure a man is your father if you don't remember how it all began. My dad died this year on Father's Day, not literally.

Thanks to his asthma medication, he still walks the earth and draws breath. I sold all my advair stock on Monday. My dad no longer exists in my world, and it would be nice to make him not exist in anyone's world. Is that blood on my sneaker?

You never want to believe your father is evil even when the evidence proves it. Evil is not a quality you learn, evil just is, and my dad just is.

Mary saw through him twenty-six years ago when she first met him. My wife has the ability to sense good and evil in people, which is why she married me. We all have the ability to some degree, but most of us fail to listen to our intuitions. The voices in my head remind me of this fact daily.

When looking in the mirror, I see goodness gazing back at me. During the past year, goodness has put on a few pounds. When looking at my father, wickedness glares back at me, and I question if he's really my flesh and blood.

When my son was born, the first person I called was my father. He lived five minutes away from the hospital, but dad couldn't make it to see his grandson because his legs were hurting. My wife and son remained in the hospital for five days, so dad's legs must have hurt real bad. The hospital does not serve beer, and my father never showed his face.

It would give me great pleasure to break the fucker's legs, but my father is driving back to Maryland with his fifth wife. There's no doubt in my mind, he killed the previous four. My dad was born a predator, and that's what they do.

His fifth wife is a member of one of the famous chicken producing families. Her children did not want her to marry my dad, but he can be very persuasive when he needs to be. I was ambivalent about the marriage, but her children were wise to be leery.

Dad's newest wife is quite old and she has inherited a large amount of money. These are my father's two favorite things, which means her days are numbered.

I like Tyson Chicken, which makes her a competitor, and allows me not to give a shit if he kills her. This time, I hope he gets caught and locked up for a long time. The thought of my dad getting fucked up the ass in prison makes me smile.

Mary and I will no longer accept phone calls from my father, it's pointless to talk to a dead person unless you have something to say.

My father has rewarded me with a lifetime of hollow memories. One of them was the time my dad and his fourth wife brought me a birthday cake already half eaten. The daughter of wife number four had a birthday two days before mine. They drove to Connecticut and bought a cake for her party, which was the right thing to do. What was left of the cake, they stuffed back into the box, and brought it to me. The cake was still fresh in the middle. Normally this would not be the right thing to do, but at least dad remembered my birthday that year.

Mary was furious and tossed the cake in the garbage. I stuck my finger in the frosting to get a little taste after my bitterness was gone.

My father is a useless old man. Rich women seem to find him attractive due to the fact he's well endowed and mechanically inclined.

Dad couldn't seem to make it to my wedding either, but that's something to be thankful for. Maybe his legs were hurting again. If there had been an open bar at the reception, he would have found a way to get there.

My father beat his wives, and all of them were afraid to talk when he was around. One of the few things I can admire about my father is his wonderful ability to influence people.

Today is the day before Father's Day, and I'm angry about having to write this long ass entry in my journal.

Again my father has irritated me, but I may as well begin at the beginning.

It all started this afternoon when dad and the chicken lady came knocking on our door. They make an odd couple like rice and beans without the hot sauce, bland.

Mary and I had just arrived home from work and we were tired, but still gladly invited them into our home. The chicken lady hugged me even though she knows I don't like being touched. She smelled like cement drying.

Next she hugged Mary as my father stood in the doorway watching. Dad's dark eyes shine like the carapace of a beetle. He reached out toward Mary, which made me want to cut off his arms with an axe. Mary hugged my father, and he looked over her shoulder expectantly at me. The message he received from my eyes was clear enough for him to maintain his distance.

We invited them to sit on our couch, even though I had my reservations, and they hadn't made any. As they settled in, I reminded Mary to disinfect the sofa after they leave. Scooter eased past their legs while giving them dirty looks. Animals can sense the inner nature of people.

My father always tells the same three stories, and they always start with, you were probably too young to remember. How could I forget? They are the only fucking stories the old bastard recites.

Dad never tells the one about tying me to a tree and throwing baseballs at me. He never tells the tale of how he broke my fingers with a butter knife while teaching me how to tell time. I still twitch every day at eleven a.m. He never talks about punching me in the eye on my birthday after he got drunk. Our memories are different, but this doesn't stop him from babbling on.

When I offered to make them some coffee, the chick-en lady declined, but dad wanted some. He is a taker, the only thing he gives is pain, sometimes it's physical and other times it's mental.

I would have liked to poison his coffee, but settled for spitting in the cup instead. It was a small victory, but that's how wars are won. Still, it left me with an empty feeling inside, like after eating Chinese food.

Dad wanted to know about hotels in the area, so I helped him look through the yellow pages while wearing gloves. He explained how they would spend the night at a hotel, and then come back on Father's Day so we could all go out for dinner.

My father said they would be waiting at our door when we arrived home from work. The tidal wave of affection rushing from this man who claims to be my dad nearly drowned me.

When he went to the bathroom, the chicken lady tried to tell Mary some secret, but he caught her before she had a chance to spill the beans. She remained silent during the remainder of the visit, which proves my dad really knows how to control his women.

Real conversation between my father and me does not exist. The skin was hanging down from his arms like mozzarella cheese, disgusting me. It made me wonder how this monster had ever been able to intimidate me.

After telling his favorite old stories and mentioning the nice weather, all conversation dried up, and they decided to leave. Dad reminded us once again about taking us out for dinner.

Mary and I walked them to their car and I felt relieved as they drove away.

The cup my father used was thrown in the trash.

Friday

Today is Father's day, and when Mary and I arrive home from work, there's no sign of my father. This should not have been a surprise, my father is the king of lies and disappointments.

Running inside the house, I check the answering machine for messages. There's one message on the machine, and it's from my father. They apparently were not able to find a hotel north of Albany, which means they won't be taking us out to dinner. They are already on their way back to the chicken farm in Maryland.

A lie is easy to recognize if you tell a lot of them yourself. I remember seeing all the vacancy signs this morning as we passed hotels on our way to work. The new technologies of the world are a wonderful thing, but people born before 1920 should not fuck with them, or they will betray you.

My father called from a cell phone to leave his message, but when he thought he had hung up, the connection remained open, and the answering machine continued to record. I could hear my father laughing and telling the chicken lady how we would be waiting a long time to go out to dinner. Hah, hah, hah. She's laughing in the background and mumbles something about how funny it is. Then my father tells the chicken lady he called before we got home so he wouldn't have to talk to us. Hah, hah, hah. Their phone finally clicks off, but not before they were betrayed by their own words.

To know something and to actually hear something is two completely different things, like sprinkles on ice cream.

I take great pride in being able to control my emotions, but still the message hurt. It was not as bad as a fork in the eye, and it didn't make me cry. My father taught me not to be a pussy.

That evening, my son called from Arizona to wish me a Happy Father's Day. His name is the same as mine, so it's easy to remember. We always end our conversations by affirming our love for each other. We don't do this during football seasons because we are men and simplicity is the best way to go.

To the best of my recollection, my father has never told me if he loves me, which is not necessarily a bad thing. At least he didn't kill me like two of my brothers, but that's an entry for another day. Ralph and I survived, and that's the important thing. It's better to leave some things alone. It makes it easier to hate someone if you are pretty sure they don't give a fuck about you.

One thing my father did teach me is to give what I get.

My father is a dead man walking, slowly.

Monday

Why do crows eat their meals in the middle of the road? Why didn't my brother die when he was pushed out of a tree? How do you know if a tumor is growing? My life is full of questions, with few answers.

Scooter had a tumor growing on the base of her tail a few months ago. The vet determined it was not necessary to remove the lump, which forced me to perform the operation myself.

The growth turned out to be a solid chunk of tissue about the size of a marble. It's stored inside a jar in the cupboard, and Mary thinks it's garlic. She continues to be amazed how it doesn't make her hand smell. Scooter was able to recover in a few days, unlike the drug addicts I work with.

Why does my car insurance go up all the time? Why can't I ever find my socks? These are some of the questions I ask myself every day. There should be a hotline for people to call and get answers.

Why does the sore on my leg attract flies? The government always comes out on top when my taxes are done. How long does it take for my payment to arrive at its destination? Does anyone touch the envelope along the way? Should I write my phone number on the outside so they can call me?

Before mailing the payment, I rub my penis on the check. It delivers a little bit of me to Mr. Government. In life you savor the small victories.

The government doesn't allow me to vote because of

my felony convictions. Depending in what state you were convicted, it may only take one felony to become disenfranchised. Felons live by a different set of rules.

If convicted felons had been allowed to vote, George Bush would not have won the election, and that would have been better for this country. You can't blame the felons for the mess President Bush gave you.

I can buy my own bread at the supermarket, but can't own a firearm. If there's a rule about borrowing one, I'm not aware of it. Felons are not allowed to leave their state without permission, but who would dare drop a dime on me.

Last month, in order to test out my theory, I drove to the state line, got out of my car and stepped from New York into Vermont. I waited for a constable to come and arrest me, but nothing happened.

I visited Vermont for thirty-six minutes and even pissed on the ground, but nobody came to take me away. After emptying my bladder, I stepped back across the border into New York before shaking off my dick.

I don't remember reading a rule saying anything about felons owning knives. Knives are more personal than guns, they allow you to express yourself artistically. Anybody can shoot a gun, but it takes an artist to properly wield a knife.

There are rules saying felons are not allowed to drink alcohol, but nobody has ever stopped me from buying beer. I brought a six pack home with me, and now I'm waiting for the police to come. If you are able to anticipate the moves of your opponents, it's easier to survive life.

When I turn on the television there's nothing mentioned regarding me. This is not a surprise, the news stations seem more interested in entertainment than in reporting what's going on in the world.

The beers are slipping down my throat easily, and I use the third one to wash down my medications. The warnings on the bottle do not scare me, it's the man in the mirror who makes me afraid. If drinking beer is bad, then why do they taste so good?

Even with the voices for company, I can still get lonely. I phone my neighbor, but he hangs up on me. That wasn't the smartest thing for him to do, I believe in reciprocity, but not right now. Finishing the last beer, I listen carefully for the command inside my head.

As I gaze out the window, there's a fat crow feasting on a splotch of an animal in the center of the road. The crow flaps a wing in my direction, and I give it the finger.

Wednesday

When the jar of peanut butter is still half full, I throw it away. You should never finish a jar because peanut butter settles, and I am unsettled. Damn Skippy.

After removing the foil cover from a new jar, I paste it on the ceiling in the closet. This helps protect my home from radio waves.

There's an ordered place for everything in my life, excluding apple scent candles. Hot wax is nice, but not when mixed with the fragrance of apples. Apples are anathema, unless you are throwing them at cows. Even apple peels are distasteful in spite of the pleasure that can be derived from peeling things.

When we were young, I used to throw apples at my brother. Ralph now works at a fruit packing plant in Florida. I take credit for helping him to focus and gain some direction for his life. It's strange how Ralph ended up packing oranges when he never liked that color.

One year at Halloween, I painted my brother's face orange, but mom managed to put the candle out before his hair caught fire. Ralph is four years younger than I, and has learned to respect his elders.

Quite a few years have slipped away since I last saw my brother. Ralph is my only living brother, the other two ended up dead. I was seven years old and Ralph was three when our brothers died. Aaron was two, and Edward was one year old. Sudden death syndrome has wrecked havoc in our family.

My brother Aaron got caught on the end of a pitchfork when my father was working in the barn. A great number of fatal accidents happen in barns, but most go unreported.

My baby brother Edward passed away in his sleep on the railroad tracks. Trains do not stop very quickly. Choo, choo. In safety class, the first thing they teach you is not to sleep on the tracks. I always thought it was unusual how they both died on the same day, but my father explained it was providence. Dad said there wasn't enough food for everybody, and that's why God took my brothers. My father buried them in our back yard, and he still had their blood on his hands when he ate supper. Throughout the meal he kept smiling at me and Ralph. Our family never mentioned Aaron or Edward after that night.

Ralph is my favorite brother, but he has moved out of state, which makes it difficult for me to see him very often. I try to call, but most of the time he doesn't answer the phone. The fruit packing plant keeps him very busy.

The last time he came to visit was five years ago. He piloted his own little aircraft which made me very proud. I always loved Ralph more than the two dead ones.

The day he flew up to visit, I reminded my brother about when we were little and he tried to fly out of a tree. Ralph's whole body started shaking, like he was a crack addict.

My brother had meningitis as a child, and sometimes he gets after-shocks. I tried to stop the shaking by hugging him tightly. When people's eyes start to bulge out of their skulls, it's time to stop squeezing. He was very emotional as a child, and this carried over into his adult life.

Ralph wasn't able to stay long, but before he left, I gave him a box of human skin left over from one of my adventures. Two walls in my cellar are papered with skin, giving them the texture of stucco.

Before my brother hopped back inside his plane that

day, he whispered in my ear about not feeling well. As a child, he was always sickly in spite of my efforts to toughen him up. It's surprising to see him live this long.

I waved goodbye, as my brother took off from the airport with the sun glinting off the plane's wing.

Was that foil reflecting?

Friday

Today is Friday, and I have been on vacation all week. Vacation is sort of like a limited retirement even when you don't go anywhere. Work sucks, just like Sarah at the bus station, but not in a bad way.

Cleaning up around the house has made me hungry. It's already one o'clock in the afternoon, and my stomach is growling. I seldom eat breakfast, so my body will appreciate lunch.

Grabbing a frying pan from the shelf, I rapidly scramble three eggs in unsalted butter. The number of eggs has nothing to do with the fact that I have three nipples.

My egg notebook is on the counter, and I mark three X's next to Friday. When my doctor asks about my monthly egg intake, I will have the necessary documentation to show him.

My doctor is a Mormon, but it's not his fault, they probably knocked unexpectedly on his mother's door. Mary claims he is a mongoloid, but this remains to be determined. Dr. Knopp does have square fingers, which can make some procedures uncomfortable.

My egg notebook was started after I got released from prison in 1975. There was no need to count eggs in prison, they weren't real, but neither were the breasts on Julio.

I like my eggs scrambled in a deep puddle of butter, and generally prefer my women on their stomach. For health reasons, I cook only egg whites, but the butter will give them a little touch of color. Egg whites are good for you, but you should never leave your children unattended around white people.

The egg yolks are never eaten, but are saved in a jar until the required amount has been collected. After seventeen yolks have been acquired, I drive into Saratoga and pour them out in the parking lot behind my bank.

My house is seventeen miles from Saratoga, there are seventeen bodies buried in my yard, and on our anniversary I always buy Mary seventeen roses. Everything in this world is set in order by God.

Turning on the radio, I flip it to the local news station while eating my eggs. The news these days is filled with so much violence, it makes pleasant listening during mealtimes.

The reporter cuts in with breaking news to inform me how a lady jumped off the overpass in Saratoga, and died after landing on the back of her head. I guess she must have been awkward. I cram a heaping spoonful of eggs into my mouth after realizing they resemble brains.

The radio announcer states, the unidentified woman was fifty-one years old. That's my exact age, and if the eggs didn't require my complete attention, I might think about joining the lady.

After checking my head for lumps, I slam my forehead into the kitchen table three times.

What if the woman changed her mind on the way down? You don't have much time for adjustments after making the leap. There might be enough time to think, Oh shit.

Should you dress up before you jump, or would it be wiser to wear old clothes if they are going to get ruined anyway. My eggs are warm and chewy, just the way I like them.

The reporter states how the woman parked her car on the overpass moments before she jumped. The police should give her a ticket, you are not supposed to park there. If you are dead, it doesn't mean you are exempt from obeying the law. My car is parked in the driveway, and it will stay there today. I'm a law-abiding citizen.

The woman was pronounced dead at Saratoga Hospital where my wife works. I hope Mary brings me back a trophy. If you are dead, why is it necessary for someone to pronounce it.

One of my shoes is unlaced, and I waste no time getting it tied back up to avoid a safety violation. It makes me wonder if the woman was wearing appropriate footwear when she jumped. Did she wave goodbye before leaping?

After finishing my eggs, I head for the bathroom to brush my teeth. There are still twenty-five teeth left in my head, which is more than most of the people in town have. Brushing my teeth gives me a few moments to consider why the lady jumped, and still leaves me time to wonder what Mary will cook for supper.

Is it considered a suicide if you intend to kill yourself? I wonder if she filled her car with gas before abandoning it on the overpass. It's always a good idea not to let your vehicle get below a half tank.

Tomorrow, I will drive into Saratoga and investigate the scene. There are too many police around the area for me to make an appearance today.

It will need to be determined what caused the lady to tumble. Egg yolks can be slippery.

Monday

My car needs to have its oil changed every three thousand miles. I need Mary to massage oil on my balls every other day, but not 5W40, that's what my car likes.

It's raining as I drive to the service station, but my windows are rolled down. The cool precipitation splatters my face and chest refreshing my soul. I'm not able to refresh myself with blood since HIV came around. Opening my mouth as wide as possible, I allow the sour rain to trickle down my throat. Rain does not taste fresh and clean anymore, due to the low pressure systems coming up from Mexico.

Nothing is the way it used to be, and it seems like control is slipping away from me. Listening to the car radio helps me remain calm if I can locate the correct station. I can hear the music playing in my head even with the volume off. The beat is the salsa rhythm of my heart.

After arriving at the station, I quickly check inside the car to make sure it's clean before my mechanic takes it. I don't want Jim to see anything he shouldn't. There's an Arizona Tea bottle half filled with urine in the door pocket, which I remove and place next to the gas pumps.

Dave is behind the counter, and he wants to know if the keys are in the car. Where else would they be? Dave is not the smartest person in the garage, but he is consistently friendly, despite having hairy arms.

I smile, it seems like the human thing to do. People have died when I have a smile on my face. It helps them on their way out of this world if the last thing they see is a friendly face. It's less traumatic for them, and it gives me a sense of accomplishment.

I take a seat in the waiting room and wait. There are newspapers and magazines set out on the table, but I don't touch them, my gloves are at home.

The garage is always busy with people coming in and out, paying for gas and buying coffee. None of the customers are wearing yellow trouser's which makes me uneasy.

Jim drives my car into the garage, and reads the note I left on the steering wheel. It's a gentle reminder for him to save the dirty oil, and put it in the plastic jugs behind the front seat. The best way to live a problem free life is to dispose of your own waste.

That's why this particular garage has been getting my business for years. You just can't beat good service, and I love these people.

They are able to complete an oil change in less than thirty minutes, which allows me enough time to run across the street to the public library and expose myself. The librarian wears thick glasses that make me appear enormous.

Jim sticks his head into the waiting room to ask about having my tires rotated. I inform him, the tires rotate as they spin. He laughs, and goes back inside the garage stall. His stupid question makes me wonder what kind of mechanic he is. The matches are still in my shirt pocket.

In less than twenty minutes, Jim backs my car out of the garage and hands Dave the keys. Why didn't he hand me the keys? Jim's behavior has a touch of rudeness to it. People make things much more difficult than they need to be.

I light a match as Jim walks past me, but he must not have enough grease on his uniform, and there are no fireworks.

Stepping up to the counter, I fumble through my wallet for a credit card. As Dave reaches out for the card, I scrape it along his hairy arm while smiling.

Tuesday

I'm sitting in my kitchen with only the voices to share my company when the pen runs out of ink. There was no warning issued by the pen before it decided to stop working. Is this some type of union work stoppage? There's no mandrel in my home, but this does not keep me from unscrewing the pen and looking inside.

The ink depot is not discernible, so I examine my pant's pockets, but they are empty. Any other time, I would love a mystery, but today there's no time for this shit. I need to make an entry in my journal, and this requires a pen that writes.

Screwing the pen back together doesn't help, it still withholds the ink. I use the pen to press into the flesh covering my temple as rage explodes behind my left eye. Somehow I am able to ignore the pain, and regain my focus. The need to determine why the pen won't write incites me to continue investigating.

Ants are crawling over my bare feet, making it difficult to remain calm, and at the same time hold onto the pen. The ants move faster, and their tiny legs are tickling me to the edge of insanity. I clamp my eyes tightly shut while taking deep slow breaths, but my hands have started trembling like a choking bird. The pen escapes my grip and drops onto the table.

The insects have suddenly ceased their movements, granting me enough courage to open my eyes. Looking at my feet, the ants have disappeared, but the paleness of my toes shocks me. Where did the ants go? When you need that voice in your head to answer a question, it's never there.

I try the pen again, but for some reason it stubbornly refuses to work. There may be more pens in the house, but I am determined to stop this rebellion right here without involving other insurgents.

Picking up the pen, I place it between the first two toes of my left foot, and again attempt to make it write. What the hell is the problem here? Stomping my foot on the floor causes the pen to shake loose and slide across the kitchen tile.

My right foot stays motionless, but I remain wary and watch it from the corner of my eye. Disregarding the pen on the floor, I massage my sore left foot. My extremity appears to have been involved in some type of trauma.

I should write a note regarding the injury in case it gets worse. There is a pen on the floor next to the refrigerator, but when I retrieve it, the instrument does not write.

Using two hands, I take it apart, but am unable to determine where the ink originates from. Closing my eyes, I reassemble the pen in less than ten seconds and place it on the table. Semper Fi.

This whole ordeal is making me confused, and my inner voices are speaking in unknown tongues. I swallow two blue vitamins with some milk in order to settle my stomach. Where are my shoes?

My vision is blurring, and there's a tingling feeling in my feet, but I can still make out the pen lying on the table.

Thank God.

If this continues, it may become necessary to call my doctor. He will need to know my symptoms, which means I should write them down. Reaching for the pen on the table, I am able to recover it with one hand. My dexterity amazes me, but the effort is to no avail because the pen doesn't write.

My eyes are watering profusely, and my hands still tremble. I dab my eyes with a slice of gluten free bread. Eating the soggy bread upgrades my condition, which proves that good nutrition leads to improved mental health.

My vision is clearing, and the sensation of pins and needles in my feet has disappeared. The voices in my head are trying to send a command, but there are too many entities speaking at the same time. They will elect a spokesman and get back to me.

Grabbing my cell phone off the kitchen counter, I call for the lottery numbers. This could be my lucky day. The recording spouts out the numbers as I attempt to scribble them down, but my pen does not write. I click off the phone in order to investigate this mind-boggler.

I endeavor to see through the pen while holding it up to the light above the sink, but the plastic is too dense. A few people have tried to see through me, and the successful ones are dead.

Calling the lottery line again, it seems like they give me the same numbers, but I can't be sure. My memory is not what it used to be, and I should learn to write things down. Capturing a pen and scrap of paper from the table, I begin to jot down the numbers, but the pen will not write.

Shutting off the phone, I disassemble the pen, but can't figure out the problem. There are no instructions inside to explain why it's empty. After examining the instrument carefully, I am unable to locate a telephone number for service. I put the pen back together and set it on the table.

Why is the phone in my hand? Where has the day gone? How did it manage to get dark so soon? The phone rings as I'm washing my hands in the sink, but I don't answer because we have caller ID.

Reaching for the pen on the table, my intent is to write down the caller's number, but the pen won't write. With the dry point, I carve the number into the flesh of my forearm, and throw the pen away.

It's remarkable how relaxing it is to recall the events of this day. This journal entry was written in my blood.

Thursday

We are having a heat wave all across the Northeast this week. It's not even noon and the sun is already beating down unmercifully. The thermometer on the side of my house reads 98 degrees, and I wonder how long it will take for something to cook in this heat.

My dog is chained to a post in the yard where there's no shade. It's not really my dog, just a stray from town that followed me home.

My neighbor is sneaking into my yard to free the dog. Yesterday, he tried to supply the dog with water, but I managed to repel his invasion. Wilbert seems to think he's a one man army of liberation, but I consider him a heathen trying to unlawfully occupy my land.

Here he is again today, attempting to loosen the dog's collar. His arm gets near the dog's face, and the beast decides to take a bite. When animals get hungry they are able to find their own sustenance.

My neighbor seems surprised by the dog's reaction to freedom, but the animal did not ask to be liberated. North Korea has no oil, and you won't discover any on my property.

Does my neighbor consider the dog a freedom fighter or a terrorist? Some things can be complicated dependent upon your point of view. A jar of gravy is five inches tall no matter how you look at it.

Leaving my air conditioned kitchen, I saunter outside

to convince Wilbert it would be prudent to retreat from my yard. Negotiation works because I'm willing to fight him in my yard so it's not necessary to fight him in his. He withdraws quickly from my land, and goes inside his house. Should I declare victory, or will history judge my results?

The doggy looks like he could use some water, but sometimes you just have to buck up.

What did my neighbor accomplish by his actions? He is injured, my land is unoccupied, and the dog remains chained to the post. When holding captives, I prefer a heavy steel chain, but not when they are around my ankles.

The dog raises its head and grins at me. The animal has some of my neighbor's blood on its teeth, but this doesn't mean we will become friends.

Now that my property is secure, it allows me to go back inside and observe the dog from my window. You have to take care of your body by not staying out in this kind of heat for extended periods of time.

I read the paper while waiting for the sun to do its work on the dog. The animal has no papers. I keep my eye on Wilbert's door in case he decides to make a surge back into my territory.

Knowing the dog is thirsty, I make myself a cup of coffee. The sun continues to bear down, causing the animal's fur to shine like my dad's church shoes. The dog flops over on its side, and I wonder if it's sick.

Wilbert comes back outside with a gauze bandage wrapped around his left arm. Is he going to try a different type of tactic? I remain in my house for a few moments in order to be fair and give his buildup a chance to work.

He looks toward my front door, and then looks at the dog. Part of the reason his invasion has been less than successful is that Wilbert lacks focus.

What in the world is he trying to accomplish? These are the times when my neighbor gets on my nerves, but I grant him life because he amuses me.

Opening my front door, I inform him the coffee is ready, and he spins and runs inside his house. It's hard to imagine how this unstable man got to be in control of his own property.

The dog whines weakly as I tap a finger on top of its skull. What the fuck is wrong with this animal? Some creatures are not very strong even when they have the support of a neighbor.

The blood has dissipated from the dog's teeth, and I wish Wilbert would come back over to visit. If you are going to occupy my land, you should have the courage to stay.

Apparently, my neighbor has decided to abandon the dog. He is the decider.

Last year, three stray dogs passed away in my yard. The Fourth of July will be here soon. That's Independence Day, but not for the dog, and not for the people who were constrained to come to this country through the Port of Charleston.

Going back inside my air-conditioned home, I continue to watch the dog through the window until all his movements cease.

Now I can hang the victory banner in front of my house.

Friday

Today is my day off, and I miss working, but hate my job. The medication is supposed to help with this, but they never give me the correct dosage. The doctors give you neurontin when they don't know what else to do.

The sun is shining brightly, and it causes me to squint as I sit in the kitchen squeezing my ball. Singular, just like the phone company. It was raining hard on the day my hamster was lost.

I use a stress ball to strengthen my fingers, and the power of my grip increases daily. You don't want things that are so difficult to catch in the first place slipping away from you.

Underneath the kitchen table there's a metal bucket half filled with sand. Every day, I thrust my fingers with extreme force into the granules until blood mixes with the dirt.

This procedure not only makes me less abrasive, but toughens my fingers. Tough fingers allow me to perform magic, and they come in handy when you least expect it.

As my neighbor is driving past my house, I wave one of my athletic fingers at him. He ignores me, but I prefer to believe he didn't see me. When he returns home, I will offer to share my insights on respect. Wilbert always takes time out to listen to me, and he remains teachable.

He has lived next door for twelve years, which is a long time. All the other people who lived near me have moved away or disappeared.

I am a sociable man, always willing to go out of my way to be of service to folks. My favorite reward is giving people an opportunity to visit another world. It's a one way trip, and its eye opening.

Thinking about my missing neighbor's disturbs me, but not enough to keep me from squeezing my ball. I alternate hands while slurping my coffee. I like Columbian coffee, and blue ribbons around a cow's neck, but not decaf or circus freaks with psoriasis. How can the snake lady have a skin rash?

Coffee is delectable with cream and sugar, but flavored coffee is abhorrent. My opinion is coffee should taste like coffee, not blueberries. I consider myself a common man with average tastes. This helps me to blend in, and appear civilized.

I like to grind my own beans, so the odor permeates the whole house. There are other things that don't smell pleasant when you grind them.

The radio is turned on, but my ears are not recording, so I drink some more coffee. My hearing has miraculously returned, but the volume is still low. Coffee is a diuretic, which allows sounds to flow into your central auditory system.

I like to listen to the Brazilian station even though my coffee is Columbian. The station broadcasts in Spanish and I can't understand a fucking thing they say, but I relish hearing the excitement in their voices.

Thanks to all the coffee, I need to make a trip to the bathroom and urinate. After saving a small amount of my urine in a cup, I pour it into Scooter's water bowl. It helps control her uric acid levels. I continue to squeeze my ball.

Last week in my cellar, I shoved three of my fingers deep into the flesh below a visitor's rib cage. The quest continued until I reached his liver, causing the man to soil himself and my work bench. While not pleased with the mess, I did revel in the whining sounds he emitted.

My probing proceeded on schedule, which allowed me to sustain the man's undivided attention. My guest managed to maintain consciousness throughout the procedure despite the excruciating pain.

His resilience was impressive, and the only disappointment was I was never able to make out what he was trying to tell me.

Powerful fingers are able to do amazing things.

Wednesday

Every six weeks, I go to the chiropractor and he adjusts my bones. Other than when he wipes his gloves on my pants, Dr. Swanson seems like a nice guy. When my back hurts, he makes it feel better without looking like my mother.

Mom could smell a little rancid in the summertime after she rubbed butter on her legs. My father liked the way it made them shine. I have never seen my chiropractor's legs, he simply smiles and takes my money.

When I woke up this morning, my intuition told me this was going to be a good day, even before I heard on the news that Strom Thurmond died. My dad's countenance is very similar to good old Strom's, and they have a great deal of other qualities in common.

In this great big world we live in a lot of decent people died today, but CNN only wants to blather on about one wasted redneck. There are lots of people besides me who will be rejoicing to see Strom taking the dirt nap. I hope he will be buried in close proximity to a black person. Often, it takes a long time for justice to kick in.

Despite the good news, my back still hurts, which means a session with my chiropractor is necessary. Dr. Swanson is always able to see me on short notice, but I never go to his office with an empty stomach.

My chiropractor told me to lift things with my legs, but my toes couldn't grip the cement bags. I ended up using my hands and arms, which gave me a backache.

I'm a tall man, and it makes the ground seem a considerable distance away. Just bending to tie my shoes can cause sciatica pain to shoot down my leg.

When I recline flat on my back, the pain is often alleviated. Bugs will crawl over your body if you attempt to do this in the park, and it tickles when they traverse into private areas.

I remember reading somewhere that lions have bugs, but my research is limited by the lack of subjects. My astrological sign is a Leo, and Mary is a Libra, not to be confused with labia, although she does have one. Libra's are balanced people, and Mary is perfectly proportioned.

My regular doctor thinks I'm unbalanced, and my chiropractor tells me I'm out of alignment. They both give me a poor overall view of myself, despite my height.

I have always found short people distasteful because they tend to get in your way. They are marvelous to sit behind at the movies, and are excellent if you need head right away, but otherwise are pretty much useless.

As a young man, I was considered compressed and the memories of those days are not pleasant. When standing next to a short person you can usually smell bourbon on their breath. Bourbon is one of my favorite things, affirming the inconsistencies of life I have to deal with on a daily basis.

Dr. Swanson is not a short man, as a matter of fact he's taller than I. Does this make me short? He wears a heavy blue lab coat that makes his shoulders slump, like the stock market after a George Bush speech.

Driving to the chiropractor is uncomfortable, there's no way to keep my back straight when seated in the car. Maybe I should have walked to his office.

Upon entering the office, the receptionist competently guides me to a comfortable table in the exam room. She's a slim dark-haired beauty with an inviting smile. Would it be wrong to ask for a happy ending?

While waiting for Dr. Swanson, I touch my tongue to the corners of the table, to determine who was in the room previously. No Russian's were here today, if my taste buds are correct.

There's a window near the table, which allows me to watch the cars speeding by while stretched out relaxing. Waiting for the doctor makes me anxious, so I briefly expose myself. There's something soothing about freeing your private areas.

Dr. Swanson enters the exam room, and pretends not to notice as I tuck away the lizard. Fortunately for him, I'm not Irish.

He has one huge hair curling out of his ear, but nevertheless we bond. He owns a Lexus, and I drive a Taurus, but we both have two feet on the ground. There truly is a brotherhood of mankind.

The spinal adjustment has relieved the pain, and Dr. Swanson informs me that an ice pack should finish it off. I was thinking more along the lines of hydrocodone, but I guess an ice pack will have to do.

After paying the receptionist, I kick the old man in the waiting room on my way out. The exercise is good for my back.

Sunday

Scooter's asshole is exactly five inches above the floor, unless she's sitting down. I have noticed we are not able to judge distances as well when we get older. Now days, I need to measure for accuracy, which forces me to keep a tape measure in my pocket.

As I'm getting ready for work, I wonder if it's possible to measure my patience. Today is Sunday, and nobody should have to work on the Lord's Day. My employer has no respect for tradition.

Backing my car out of the driveway, I'm thankful God did not strike me dead. Is it possible, He doesn't know how to wire a car bomb?

Pushing the cigarette lighter in and turning off the radio, I hum to myself. The lighter pops out, and it vaguely reminds me of Enrique's eye on the end of a pencil. Enrique made the sixth grade seem like medical college. When eyes are outside the sockets, they are bigger than you think, like my Nurse Manager's breasts.

As I touch the lighter to the plastic dashboard, it begins to smolder. I inhale the acrid smoke deep into my lungs, turn my head to the side and cough. The smoke from the plastic is making me dizzy, so I pull over and park in front of the strip mall. There are no strippers this morning.

The sign in the window of Video World states they are looking for employees. How can this be if they are closed? Looking at the sign carefully, it actually reads Now Hiring. How can you hire anyone if you are closed? I don't like liars, especially on a Sunday.

There are seven birds perched on a telephone wire across the street adjacent to my location. I'm already late for work, but inside me is a compelling urge to monitor the birds.

Feeling wild and free, I remove all my clothes and wait to see if the birds will react. They stare at me with their beady little eyes, but I can't determine if they are impressed.

It's impossible for me to accurately judge how far away they are, and my tape measure won't reach. Glancing down, I notice all my clothes folded on the passenger seat. I'm naked for the world to see. How did I manage to get out of the house in this condition? I dress quickly, trying to preserve my decorum.

Three of the birds on the wire fly away, and I concentrate on them until they are out of sight. Were they vultures?

The other four birds follow them, and it leaves me feeling abandoned. You can attempt to follow a bird, but success is rare, they are quick.

I have been parked at the strip mall for quite a while, and a police car has cruised by twice. This is suspicious, and I wonder who warned the birds.

I'm parked behind the local bank, but there are no egg yolks on the pavement. Somebody did a superb job of cleaning up the area. The policeman pulls up alongside my vehicle, causing me to begin the exercise of appearing human. Egg yolks run, but I don't.

Without smiling, I roll down my window and offer to shake the policeman's hand. The friendly officer wants to know if I need some help. What kind of question is that? This is probably some form of entrapment. I tell him the birds have flown away, and I'm late for work. The officer responds by instructing me to move on. Mom always told me not to dwell on things for too long.

During the drive to work, I envision boiling the policeman in a tub of vinegar. Overhead two of the birds are following me.

Tuesday

On the way to the store, I stop at a red light, and there's a blind lady standing on the corner. She has a seeing eye dog at her side, otherwise the dog would be blind too.

The dog starts to guide her across the street, but the

woman yanks the harness and pulls him back onto the curb. This is confusing. If she's blind, how can she command the dog not to cross. I wonder if the poor dog is as troubled as I am.

There's no traffic coming from either direction, and they easily could have made it across. Did the dog start to cross the street prematurely after getting hot paws?

The animal makes another attempt to lead her forward, but once more she jerks him back. If there were hairs on the back of my neck, they would be wet. Is the dog a disgruntled employee? Who is leading the parade?

The light has turned green, so I drive through the intersection and park beside the curb. This will enable me to continue watching this little drama unfold.

The dog tries once again to lead her across the street, and this time the woman follows. Three strikes and you are out. As they pass in back of my parked car, I observe the pair in the mirror. The dog grins at me, but the lady doesn't. This causes a wave of affection to flow through my body into the dog.

Maybe the lady thinks the dog can't be trusted to make major decisions. After all, how the hell does an animal know where to go?

Exiting my car, I follow them on foot, checking every so often behind me to make sure nobody is following. I scrape my foot across the sidewalk in order to cover my tracks. Sometimes the trackers are invisible.

The lady and the dog stop at the corner, and I glide up to stand beside them. The dog raises his head and stares at me. The animals piercing black eyes send commands into my brain. The dog's voice comes through clearly even though he uses broken English.

When I look boldly into the woman's face, she doesn't appear to notice, but it's hard to ascertain with the dark glasses. If she would just smile a little, her pinched facial expression might become attractive.

My eyes are reflected back at me from the lens of her glasses, and they make me afraid. One of the eyes winks at me, trying to divert my attention from the dog.

Glancing at the dog again, I concentrate in order to comprehend the instructions. The pooch smiles at me, and imperceptibly nods its head. The woman doesn't seem to notice.

There is drool hanging from the corner of the animal's mouth, and there's some froth on the edge of my lips. Too much medication this morning? The dog licks, and I swipe, which illustrates how people are more sanitary than animals.

A car is coming down the street, but it doesn't appear to be traveling very fast. The dog starts moving across the road, dragging the woman along. The car is speeding up, and it's closer than I thought.

Stepping quickly into the street, I sprint forward and trip the lady, which causes her to release the dog's harness as she falls. My first inclination is to rescue the dog. I'm a humanitarian, but I will eat chicken and fish on certain occasions.

Brakes are squealing behind me, but I don't turn around, I abhor violence. The scent of burnt rubber makes me intuitive, and I inhale deeply. This sixth sense is telling me to leave the area.

The dog is standing beside me, and he explains how the car hit his companion, and it doesn't look good. This animal really knows how to get to the point.

A crowd is gathering, which tells me it's time for a quick getaway. As I walk the dog away from the throng, he gazes into my eyes adoringly and praises me on a job well done.

There's a siren wailing in the distance, which is my signal to move faster. The pooch and I trot back to my car. I question the doggy about coming home with me, and the animal nods affirmatively.

This is the fourth dog I have adopted this summer.

Friday

After masturbating five times this morning, my body is completely exhausted, and I wonder if it could be some type of record.

I tried to aim and shoot my spunk at Scooter, but she blinked. When I was younger, my ejaculation would knock her down, but now it just makes her fur sticky. Cotton candy? Scooter's fleas probably don't appreciate my hard work.

Masturbating tends to make me sleepy, but today is the Fourth of July, and the parade has already started. The parade goes right past my house, which gives me a ring side seat. If there had been time to set up a Kool Aid stand, we could have had another Jonestown.

There are plenty of war veterans in the parade, and most of them have some type of limp. The band with the big drums has stopped right in front of my house, and when I sit on the edge of my lawn chair, the pounding instruments rattle my balls. It's like two Irish dancers kicking their heels against the side of my sack, and it causes me to salute the band.

There aren't any clowns in the parade, but there are several politicians which are almost the same thing. The only difference is clowns are professionals.

It's blistering hot today, causing huge blue flies to come out and hover around the old people. You are about two steps from death when you start drawing flies.

My neighbor is standing quietly on his porch, concentrating his attention on the parade. Using my knuckles, I tap out an SOS signal on the deck railing. Wilbert does not acknowledge receiving the message, which makes me wonder if he's a true patriot.

After the parade is finished, the town always has a picnic in the park. There are games for the children, varieties of foods for sale, and the annual volleyball contest is the highlight of the day Country people can do some strange shit. I have never been to the picnic because the people from town are peculiar, and volleyball is boring unless you can play naked on a bed of nails.

The final band is in front of my house, and the blasting horns cause my heart to skip a beat. It brings back memories of my school days.

My father forced me to take up the clarinet, so I could play in the high school band. I never learned how to play the instrument with any degree of success, but when the band marched it put me in a good position to watch the ass of the girl ahead of me.

My band instructor was well aware that my skills were inadequate, but I still managed to convince him to allow me to remain a band member. Even as a youth, the gift of persuasion exuded from me. Marching in the band was entertaining, but the clarinet sucked.

After my father found out I wasn't really playing, he burned the clarinet and proceeded to burn me with the left over charred metal parts. There is a scar in the shape of the F key on the side of my neck.

The parade is finished, and Wilbert is looking over in my direction. I wave, and go inside to take a nap.

Saturday

It's Saturday and my employer is expecting me to work today. It's an extra day for me, which means they will pay me overtime, but somehow this incentive is not enough to make me happy.

I have never worked an extra day before, nor have I ever been found standing naked under a bridge. I am more than willing to try new things, but working on a Saturday sucks, and this will never happen again.

Working at a drug and alcohol rehab could best be described as participating in a circus for malcontents. I work on the detox unit, where most of the nurses have small feet, except for Linda. She orders special shoes from Mexico.

We don't really detox anyone, instead we retox them. We exchange their drug of choice for our drug of choice, which is extremely profitable for the company.

All day long I work with addicts, which is the politically correct term for crackheads. Unfortunately, when you take away the reality, it also takes away the responsibility.

I admit deriving pleasure from hurting people, and accept the responsibility for that. There's no responsibility taken by drug addicts, they are taught all day long it's not their fault. Addicts are allowed to blame their mother, brother, job, uncle, society, car, father, and any other person or thing, just so long as they don't fault themselves.

Addicts in the new age of psychobabble are taught they have a disease which can be contained, but not cured. Cancer is a disease, high blood pressure is a disease, diabetes is a disease, but pumping heroin into your veins is not.

A person who has cancer can't simply decide they don't have it, but an addict still has a choice of not shooting that shit up or sucking on the pipe stem. It may be an extremely difficult and painful decision, but it's a choice nonetheless.

If a substance abuser, the politically correct term for a dope fiend uses heroin, we replace the heroin with methadone. Methadone is a more addicting substance, and considerably more difficult to withdraw from, but once again it's a monster money maker.

We have become the legal drug dealer for thousands of people, and the company I work for makes millions of dollars in profits every year. This business of recovery is also very lucrative for the pharmaceutical companies, and I own some of their stocks. Is that a conflict of interest?

The methadone helps the junkies to withdraw from heroin, and when that's not enough to keep them comfortable, we throw in a little ativan chaser. Whatever happened to no pain, no gain? We try to keep our patients snowed during their entire stay.

It makes their 28 days go by faster, and our days go

by easier. A junkie jonesing, bitching, and complaining or a patient nodding and sleeping. Which would you prefer? After all, it's not like they are trying to cure anybody here.

Patients tell us, if you keep me comfortable for 28 days, I can do this program. Being comfortable means snowed on our narcotics and psych medications.

Many of our patients shoot up heroin or use cocaine during their whole length of stay. It's not hard to smuggle drugs into a rehab.

If patients are caught in the act of using, our managers may discharge them depending on the census. If there are empty beds in the building, nobody will be kicked out, this is a profit business.

I suggested they should open one unit for the patients who wanted to continue using drugs during their stay.

This way it would give the few patients who are really seeking recovery, the opportunity not to be influenced by the ones here for their own agenda.

Due to the effectiveness of our program 89% of our patients return to alcohol and drugs, and then return to us. This is called job security. Repeat business is our specialty. Another 5% of our patients leave treatment and die. This is called relapse prevention. Another 5% are never heard from again, which leaves us with a 1% recovery rate. Recovery is elusive, like finding a snails ass.

If we were in any other type of business, this level of inefficiency would cause us to close, unless we were subsidized by the Federal Government.

They have quite a few ineffective teaching programs at this facility. I wanted to start a Shoot One - Teach One Program, but was told it would cut down on our repeat business. I love this job.

I honestly believe everybody deserves a chance. You should be allowed one year to get your shit together and become a productive member of society, or at least not a burden. At the end of one year, if you have failed to accomplish this goal, you would be killed and gently planted in a hole. This would be our Off the Dole or In the Hole

Program. This seems like a fair opportunity, but I'm nonjudgmental.

That's why I agreed to work an extra day today, and why it will never happen again. This whole situation makes me angry, but it's nothing a couple of xanax won't cure.

My next job will be on a cancer ward, where the people are really sick, and they won't try to steal my sneakers.

Monday

This morning, I heard on the radio about a local man being killed by a cow. I live in a rural area, and there's not much of anything here except cows. You don't get the opportunity to hear this kind of news in the big city.

Everybody in town will be gossiping about the man who was murdered by a cow, You can't even make this shit up. Many questions go through my head, I'm naturally inquisitive.

Will the cow be charged in the death of the man? Was the attack premeditated? The radio stated, the man had been attempting to load a cow on his truck when the animal suddenly pushed against him crushing his chest. What the fuck?

If the man nudged the cow first, will the animal be able to plead self defense? I wonder if the cow is remorseful about committing the crime. Do cows have a conscience? Did the beast drool on itself after killing the man? The radio never seems to give you enough information.

It makes me curious about what the man's family will write on his grave marker. Here Lies Edgar, Crushed By A Cow. It has a nice ring to it.

I wonder if the cow had always been pushy, or was this a one time event. Was the animal troubled as a calf? Where were the cow's parents when this happened? Could they have possibly prevented this?

Did the cow have a history of violence? Has anybody

heard of domesticated bovine depression? Was the cow on any medications? Hormones? I have so many questions, and there are so few answers.

There's a herd of cows on the farm across the road from my house. This is going to demand closer attention from me. I never realized they are such menacing animals, they always appear so docile. Chewing and plotting, plotting and chewing. Apparently, they are just waiting for the right moment to make their move.

I wonder if the cow was ever sexually abused, and as uncomfortable as the question may be, it deserves to be answered. The cow did not crush the man without a good reason. Did the man touch the udder? Cows have enormous eyes, and they don't miss much.

Did the animal focus on the man's face when it pulverized him? If the man is survived by any children, I feel sorry for them. My dad was killed by a cow, just does not sound right.

Nobody mentioned what type of truck the man was using, maybe the cow resented foreign vehicles. Could the animal have been involved with drugs? Blood should be drawn in order to determine if the cow was sober. Can the animal be charged with Crushing While Intoxicated?

Cows tend to walk funny, and I wonder if the man mocked the animal until it couldn't take it anymore. In some countries the cow is Holy, but not here. In this country the cows push back.

I wonder if there were any other animals in the area when the incident happened. Left unchecked, this could be the beginning of a cow rebellion. Will cows gather in herds to gossip about the killing?

The cow may be assigned a public attorney, so they better have read the animal its rights. Did the cow endeavor to moo after it killed the man? Will the animals have a protest march about unfair working conditions? Justice for the cow. It makes me feel like doing a little marching myself.

One fact I know from studying the subject is cows don't march very well, which means they will have to ride in a truck.

Who's the lucky fucker that's going to load them?

Wednesday

Mary sent me on a mission to buy a loaf of bread. Stewart's Mart is five minutes from our house, meaning there's an excellent opportunity to make my wife grateful. Women who are grateful do pleasing things. After buying the loaf and tossing it in the car, my attention is drawn to the red brick building across the street.

The windows are boarded up, and nailed to the cracked wooden door is a sign that reads AVAILABLE. What does this mean? The building is abandoned, and it leaves me wondering what could be available.

Nobody is standing outside the building for me to ask, but there's a phone number printed on the lower right corner of the sign. My adventurous spirit wants me to investigate, so I need to find a phone.

My cell phone has been destroyed after hearing on the news they can cause cancer. My mom died of cancer, and they say the disease runs in families. It's too bad the big C didn't run into my father. The worst problem he ever had was a case of athletes feet, but my dad was a grease monkey, not an athlete.

I can remember how dad would gouge out the oily crud from between his cadaverous fingers with a butter knife after he got home from work. Frisky would lick the fresh scrapings off the floor, and then try to slobber on me. I never did like that dog.

Mom didn't burrow at her cancer, it was in her brain. The surgeon excavated the tumor, but he left a chunk behind, and I always wondered why he didn't take it all. It's like not being able to eat a whole pie in one sitting unless it's cherry.

Nobody told me what kind of cancer mom had, but it was the killer kind. I'm pretty sure my father transmitted it to her. Dad gave our family loads of things, and none of them were good, except for the blue bicycle he gave Ralph on my birthday. My gift was a punch in the eye.

My brother let me ride the bicycle when our father wasn't looking. Dad always liked Ralph best because he was an ass kisser.

I should phone my brother, but first I need to call the number on the sign and see what's available. After finding a pay phone, I slide in the coins, and dial the number.

On the third ring, a woman from Peal Realty answers the phone. I explain to her how they have a sign posted, and I was wondering what was available. The woman wants to know what I'm interested in, but the answer to her question would force the conversation in an unhealthy direction. Instead, I explain to her about the AVAILABLE sign with her phone number on it.

She demands to know where the sign is located, and it leads me to believe I'm conversing with an idiot. After suggesting that she should get tested for dementia, I question her about why she can't remember where they put the sign up. She informs me, the agency has signs placed all over the city.

This is turning out to be more complicated than scratching my nuts through corduroy. My focus is starting to drift toward the hooker across the street, as the realtor repeats her question about the location of the sign. I recognize the exasperation in her voice, and it causes me to weep.

After waiting a few moments to get my emotions under control, I start to ask another question, but the drone of a dial tone is coming from the phone. We must have lost our connection, and I should call her back, but my interest has waned.

Mary is going to be wondering what's taking me so long, which means the possibility of me receiving a sexual favor has vanished.

While hopping into my car, I notice my shoes are wet.

Friday

The Bluegrass Festival is back again this year, just like my sister's herpes. It's held right across the street from where I live. The Festival, not my sister.

Country music sucks, and bluegrass music could best be described as country music on speed. It's like a Ku Klux Klan musical.

The music, if you dare call it that, began at dawn with a cacophony of fiddles. It sounded like somebody was scraping their fingernails over a blackboard, and it caused my cat's legs to tremble until she pissed herself.

Scooter looks up at me, pleading with her eyes, and I can usually hear her voice in my head, but today she has decided to speak English, and it's laborious to understand.

After locating an interpreter inside my skull, it becomes clear that Scooter feels the noise coming from the Festival sounds like wolves and she's afraid.

Some wolves are gray in color, as are the people at the Festival. My washer is new, and I wonder if this is a coincidence.

There is an innate need within me to observe the Festival folk in greater detail, but I can't remember where my binoculars are.

Holding Scooter up to the window is a waste of time, but I do it anyway. During the last month, most of her vision has faded, and she can't see anything. The sun shines down on the milky glaze covering her eyes, and I hope she can smell the folks from the Festival. The odor is similar to mild cheddar cheese.

There's urine on the kitchen floor, and I can't imagine how it got there. After examining myself, I find my shirt is wet. This information is interesting, but only for a moment, my mind wanders like Grandma used to.

There must be two hundred travel trailers parked in the field, and I wonder where they relocated the cows. Where the hell is a tornado when you need one? There's not a cloud in sight. I pour some table salt into my palm, hoping it will cause the sky to darken. The trick always seemed to work for mom, but dad complained about her dry hands.

I pour Fruit Loops over the urine on the floor, it's great for soaking things up. If you use it to clean up blood, it makes all the loops cherry red.

The binoculars are still missing, but I did manage to find my wife's scope. The folks from the Festival appear close enough to touch. Magnifying these people makes me question evolution.

The music continues to blare across the field into my home, and it makes me feel violated. People are actually trying to dance to this shit.

It looks like Scooter is dehydrated, so I pour some Gatorade in her bowl. She likes the blue kind even though her bowl is brown. Animals have no sense of clashing colors.

Looking through the scope helps me see the revelers with clarity when I squint. It's dangerous to look at white people with your eyes wide open, the glare can cause blindness in humans.

I found the scope attached to Mary's rifle in the closet. She does not like me to touch her weapon, but I'm granted permission to touch her on occasion. As soon as I manage to focus the scope on somebody, they topple over. This is turning out to be a lot of fun.

The bluegrass music has ceased, and the Festival go-ers are running to and fro in panic. I hope none of them fall and break a hip.

Scooter is looking much better, and I believe she gazes at me with love, but there's no way to be sure due to her blindness.

I can hear sirens headed in the direction of the Festival.

Monday

I ran to the time clock, but was still fifteen minutes late punching in for work. The minutes were lost while I was smoking weed in the parking lot. It was just enough to settle my nerves, they have been frazzled lately. When you are on the anxiety highway, self medication is the only route to take. The weed leaves me feeling buoyant, like my Nurse Managers breasts.

They have a dining hall here at work, and the staff is allowed to eat there as well as the patients. In some ways we all suffer equally. You can buy a meal ticket for two dollars, which allows you to get everything on the menu. If you just want a salad or one item, the price is one dollar. It's like asking if you would like a mild case of stomach cramps or severe diarrhea for the next six months.

It's good to have choices rather than all your options being taken away. There are times I want to poke out the cook's right eye, but I have the option to choose the left one. Decisions, decisions, just like the magazine.

While walking to the detox unit, I glance out the window and notice one of the kitchen employees standing outside the rear entrance. He seems to be searching for something. Could it be his missing chromosome? Life is a mystery.

The kitchen worker perturbs my soul, and makes me question my faith. I never believed in evolution until this very moment. I may have discovered the missing link. He enters the building, and I wait expectantly for the magic show to begin.

When I place my palm against the window pane, it feels cold. Exiting the building allows me to realize it's even colder outside, and my hopes of becoming a meteorologist vanish.

Maybe I should have grabbed my coat, but slipping my arms into the sleeves arouses me. Who needs viagra when wool is available?

Walking to the entrance where the kitchen worker was last seen, I place my face against the cold metal door and inhale the remnants of his presence. Digging with my finger deep inside my ear, I scoop enough wax to smear the number three on the door handle.

Now the planets are in alignment, and so are my testicles. The cold is beginning to seep into my bones, like a parasite. I return inside the building, and the warm moist air makes me gag.

Our unit is being called for lunch on the overhead paging system. I never eat lunch in the facility, my longevity depends upon it.

My half hour lunch period is spent hiding in one of the doctor's offices, where I masturbate furiously. Over the years, nobody has noticed my lunchtime activity, except for the housekeeper when she mops the floor.

If still employed at this facility three years from now, I will stop hiding and become more approachable.

As the patients come back onto the unit from lunch, I emerge from the office like a butterfly from its cocoon.

How did the stain get on my shoe?

Wednesday

The weatherman warned us about dangerous high winds for today. Looking out my kitchen window, I can see the stop sign across the street swaying back and forth, and I wish someone was blowing me.

Mary is shorter than I even when we are sitting in the car, which means the sun never shines in my eyes. I love my wife's purity, but she's not white. White people should be considered a danger to society. When you look at them during daylight hours it can damage your retinas.

I have an enormous amount of pride for having eliminated all the Caucasians from my family, except for myself. Every family needs a token, and this is my role to play. My work is done on this earth, yet my body remains a pasty white color, as does my semen. During the winter months my spunk will turn a shade of white that unsettles me. Last year at Thanksgiving, I drank a container of red food coloring, but it didn't help.

This world is a curious place, and so is the little town I reside in. Living in a small town is convenient because when people disappear nobody notices, and when you sleep with your cousin nobody cares. Small town life is often not worth living.

Scooter is rubbing her furry head against my leg. Her ass is exactly four inches from the floor when she is standing. It used to be five inches, but she inherited a hunchback.

I hear the mail truck coming down the street, and close my eyes. I have never seen the mailman, and somebody will die if that happens. There will be no witnesses.

The truck's horn is beeping, as I carefully feel my way out onto the deck while keeping my eyes tightly shut. The breeze is ruffling the hairs on my thighs, affirming my decision not to shave today.

A voice from nowhere states my mail is here, and I hold my hands out in front of me expectantly. Letters are placed in my hands, as the voice questions me about my health status.

Nosey people annoy me. I suggest the voice should mind it's own business. A door slams, and I can hear the mail truck pulling out of my driveway. It's too bad the President couldn't make the same decision.

Opening my eyes, it's a shock to realize I'm standing naked on the deck. Being modest, but also well hung, I spend a few moments admiring myself. What has happened to my clothes? Have there been other robberies in the neighborhood? Before a crowd can gather, I run inside the house.

As I'm placing the mail on the kitchen counter, the phone starts ringing. The ringer reverberates in my head like bells, and reminds me of the Christmas when my brother got burned. The answering machine catches the call, but whoever was trying to contact me doesn't leave a message.

This makes me angry, and I pinch Scooter's ear.

I have a gut feeling it was my father calling, but he's a dead man to me. It's not healthy to talk to dead people, and it's not healthy for live people to converse with me.

My car is pulling into the driveway, and this astounds me. It makes me thankful to be alive in such a magical world, and I wait anxiously to see who will vacate the car. It's Mary, which means this was not really magic.

It's no longer blustery outside, and the world is safe.

Thursday

Most people who reside in the United States believe we live in a great country. Country music makes me distressed, but country fried chicken is good. Bird flu is bad. Just think how great this country could be if we didn't try to hold people back.

The government needs to be able to subordinate the masses. There are a great number of tools they employ in order to bring control and containment to fruition.

My mom had several masses on her brain, and they could not be controlled or contained. The Grim Reaper runs free. Death is an old friend, and when my time comes, I will embrace it.

Sometimes death can become orgasmic, but usually not when it's your own. Being a reserved man, I try to contain myself, but some days it's difficult to control myself. When you can no longer maintain self control, people will come and take you away. I accept no substitutes.

They dragged me away to a farm once, but nothing grew there. They taught me how to ride a horse, but not how to stare one down. Horses have enormous eyes, and other parts.

This country is the land of great opportunity, a place where many have sought refuge. Some folks entered through Ellis Island on their way to freedom. You should never push when you are in line. They came here for freedom, and a chance to be whatever they wanted to be.

I keep a lock on my shed, but people were not locked up on Ellis Island unless they pushed in line. There's no excuse for rudeness. Always make sure the ladies go first so you can stare at their bottoms.

There are always two sides to every story unless you are bipolar. Some people came to this mighty land of freedom through the Port of Charleston, a different perspective even if you only have one eye. They came not of their own volition, but because they were forced here to be used, abused, and sold in the marketplace. Capitalism is what made this country great.

God is great, and he sees the sins of a nation. Some day there will be a day of reckoning, but probably not today. We do indeed live in a wonderful country, ask an Indian, if you can find one.

People like to say all those things were in the past, and it's a new day. Good point. Now the government uses social status, economics, and prisons in order to contain and control. Nothing has really changed. Old rich white men maintain all the power. Many of them can't control their bladders, yet they control the major corporations, and our government is run by the large corporations of this country.

This makes me so angry, I squeeze my testicles, but there has to be a better way for me to express my rage. I release my nuts before the people who watch me think I'm crazy. I can feel their eyes on me, and this time it's not the horse.

This is a great country, but think how remarkable it could be if we didn't try to hold people back.

Saturday

Mary and I are flying on a plane, although actually we are inside the plane, and its flying. Don't get it twisted.

I wanted to mark my seat so everybody on the plane would know it's mine, but my wife wouldn't allow it. She inhibits my fun levels, but it's gratifying not to have to search for a sex partner every night.

Before we boarded, Mary gave me a list of things I would not be permitted to do during the flight. Putting the Mark of the Beast on my seat was one of them. My wife knows me far too well, but there still might be some surprises reserved for her.

The seats on the plane are small, I'm a massive man, and these two facts point toward an uncomfortable flight. My knees are jammed into the seat in front of me, and its becoming increasingly painful. The plane must have been designed by a midget.

Unbuckling my seatbelt, I stand up and move boldly to the center of the aisle. Some of the other passengers are starring at me, but that's normal. As a role model, it does not bother me when people gawk.

I'm determined that nobody can force me to sit back down in the cramped seat. There are sixty-four eyes observing me, and this seems like far too many, but I'm not a mathematician.

The flight attendant asks me to sit down, but I demand to know why. I always question authority, and am not in the habit of being intimidated. The stewardess explains how the seat belt light is on, and I need to remain in my seat until it goes off. What the fuck is this, some kind of magic show?

My anger is reaching a crescendo as I look to Mary for support, but she has her hands covering her face. That leaves sixty-two eyes still watching me. I'm not an elephant, but it's burdensome to remember all of my wife's rules.

I'm conciliatory when returning to my seat, hoping to pacify the stewardess in order to catch her unawares. The flight attendant smiles and thanks me. I respond with a fuck you, but only in my mind. The seat is cramping my freedom of speech.

Before we left the house this morning, Mary forewarned me about Sky Marshals aboard the plane. Why she thought, it was necessary to pass on this tidbit of information is beyond my ability to comprehend. If the plane is not in the air, do they become regular marshals? I meditate on the mysteries of life while continuing the notations in my journal.

The little boy sitting in front of me is making horrendous noises. This is rude, and age can never be an excuse for bad manners.

Opening my bag of peanuts, I dump them over the brat's seat and wait anxiously to see if the kid is allergic. The little blue eyed wonder is not showing any harmful effects, instead he's screaming and laughing even louder than before.

The boy's parents seem to be encouraging this obnoxious behavior. I wish the claw hammer was inside my carry on luggage.

The parents of the child are glaring at me, and their body language seems threatening. My mouth smiles, but my eyes don't. The mentally defective parents manage to get the boy quieted down without me having to say one word. You can communicate a lot of things by using your eyes.

Looking out through the small circular window next to my seat, I can see billowy white clouds hanging in the sky. They remind me of the pillow I used to smother a guy in Schenectady. Licking the window, I ascertain the cloud's taste just like motor oil. This is more proof that the environmentalists are right.

I glance around to see if anyone has noticed me, but it appears nobody is looking. Mary continues to hold her head down, and I encourage her to do this whenever we are together. She will never be forced to testify in court. She's an exceptional wife, and the only one I have.

The pilot is explaining over the intercom how we are preparing to land. It makes me wonder what kind of clown is flying the plane. What is there to prepare? We either land or we don't. I allow myself three swallows of water, and no more, I'm a conservationist.

The flight attendant struts down the aisle in order to

make sure we are all buckled in. It makes me feel warm and fuzzy knowing how much they care about my safety. The stewardess glances at my belt twice, as she notices the tent I pitched in my pants.

As we disembark, I wonder why the police are here.

Wednesday

My wife and I are vacationing in Arizona, and I have noticed that everything dries faster in the desert. We are staying in Tucson, and the air is extremely dry, but my ass is not. Mary is downstairs in the hotel lobby, waiting for me to take her to breakfast, but I'm sitting here on the toilet wiping my ass. It's difficult to write in my journal at the same time.

There must be other people besides me who are forced to take time out and wipe their ass. It's one of those private subjects nobody wants to talk about.

When I was young, it took one wipe and the dirty job was completed. The paper would be dry as a bone, but now I have to wipe over and over again. Finally, just when I think my ass has run dry, I discover more shit on the paper. This is disgusting.

I consider killing myself, but the urge quickly passes as I continue to wipe. Will Mary accept this as an excuse for me being late for breakfast? Why can't I manage to wipe myself clean without taking so long? Am I this full of shit?

Maybe this is what happens when you get older. If this is what the future involves, I want no part of it. I wipe some more. What if this never stops? Could the world end while I sit on the toilet?

My stomach is growling with hunger, but there's nothing to eat in the bathroom. Apparently this is not a five star hotel.

There are several splotches of blood on one of my sneakers. Maybe it's caused by the hemorrhoids, but there's no blood smeared on the paper even though on previous days there has been.

Blood soothes the soul when it's daubed on the snow, but not when it's on your toilet paper. I wipe one more time, and it looks like we are almost there. Mary is probably starving by now.

Wiping can be tedious work, and I wonder if fasting would help me avoid this. As a medical technician, I could give myself a colostomy, but the surgery should never be performed when you are on vacation. I could practice the procedure on someone else while we are in Tucson.

I keep six tea bags in my back pocket to help stop blood flow. Sometimes when you cut people, they bleed out too quickly, but when you place the tea bags over cuts, it stanches the bleeding. Tannins can extend your fun time, and afterwards you can use the bags to make a wonderful red zest tea.

I wipe once more, and it's good enough for me. Standing up on shaky legs, I begin to wash my ass. We really are more evolved than monkeys, but there must be an easier way to do this. My lower legs have no feeling, but when I look down they are still there. The numbness must be from sitting on the damn toilet for so long.

My ass is finally clean, I wash my hands and say my prayers. I count my fingers, and today there are ten. With my butt hole refreshed, it's time to get downstairs and meet Mary.

Her breakfast is going to be a little late, this day had a shitty start.

Saturday

Death is the final act of living, it's like being the last person off the bus, usually you are tired, sweaty, and ready to go.

Death is inevitable even though some people fight very hard to avoid it. I embrace death, it's like hugging a big loaf of warm bread without the calefaction.

Sometimes I rush to meet death. On the way to work this morning, I got my car up to 100 mph on a straight stretch of highway. I held my head out the window, but death did not take my breath away. This was somewhat disappointing because annihilation would have been better than going to work.

As my head was out the window, the wind dragged my lips away from my teeth, and made me into a horse. The air flowing over my face was invigorating, like soaking your feet in warm blood. It's important to maintain blood at the proper temperature. It thickens if allowed to cool too quickly, and then becomes difficult to get out from under your toe nails.

Today is Saturday, and you should never have to work on the weekends. It's like going against God. Don't die on a weekend or they will just stick you in a corner until Monday. It would be like having sex, but you can't cum. What's the point?

Some folks prefer to meet the Grim Reaper on their own terms by committing suicide. Personally, I believe suicide is a fundamental right everyone has, but few people take advantage of.

My only suggestion would be, if you are really going to kill yourself don't tell anybody. Don't spoil the surprise for everyone. Try to remember the Nike commercial slogan.

During my childhood, contact with leather would cause me to break out in a rash, but that didn't stop me from enjoying hamburgers. Revenge is sweet, but you can't achieve it if you are dead, unless you are getting even with yourself.

Scooter is 22 years old and she's dying, but she doesn't make a point of telling everybody. She does piss on the floor, and some actions speak for themselves.

The sun rose today, and so did I. Not bad.

Monday

Once every year I need to get a physical, and it's that time again. I call my doctor, but he never answers the phone, which can be disconcerting. Mom always told me, just put one foot in front of the other and everything will work out.

A nurse answers on the second ring, and instructs me to come into the office this afternoon. I don't have a problem coming, but getting it up is difficult due to my high blood pressure. I tell the nurse this afternoon will be fine.

Some people have to make an appointment to see Dr. Knopp, but not me. After my first trip to his office, he left specific instructions with the staff to get me right in whenever I call.

After taking a shower, I soak my genitals in a special solvent for five minutes and then dry off. It's never a good idea to stay wet for long periods of time, or your parts get wrinkled. It helps me understand why whales try to commit suicide by beaching themselves.

There's an evil looking bald headed old man peering from my mirror. Is this character trying to seduce me? I have seen him somewhere before, but can't conjure up where. It could have been the post office.

Getting dressed makes me thankful that I'm still able to perform the function. As usual, I'm running a little late, but the doctor will wait for me. After grabbing a soda from the fridge, I run out the door.

There's a brand-new car parked in the driveway. This is the first car I have ever owned that wasn't blue. Change is good, unless you are sitting in the yard at Attica. My new car is gray, the same color as old white people.

The doctor's office is only ten minutes from my house, but the time can change depending on how fast I drive. I like to be precise.

After finishing my soda, I toss the can out the window. A five-cent deposit is not enough to conquer my rebellious heart. My free nature causes me to weep with joy, and I lick the salty tears running down my cheeks. My tongue is very long, and some people consider this feature admirable. Mary does.

Arriving at the doctor's office, I always park in the reserved spot in order not to waste time. People don't realize how special I am. Remaining in the car for a brief moment allows me to collect my thoughts, which can be difficult. A few of them hide in the corners, but its rewarding to hunt them down, it's like getting sand out of a cat's ass.

After entering the office, I check in with the cute blond nurse at the reception desk. There are no people in the waiting area, which makes me wonder what they call it when nobody is waiting. I would normally question the nurse, but she doesn't appear overly intelligent. She's probably just an LPN, not a real nurse.

The imitation nurse informs me the doctor will see me now, and leads me into a closet where I take a seat. It's not really a closet, but the exam room is small enough to be one.

As far as I know Dr. Knopp is not gay, but it wouldn't disturb me if he was. Mary thinks he's a mongoloid, but I believe he's simply an odd looking Caucasian. I have failed to conquer my aversion to white people, but I'm trying to get more in touch with myself.

The doctor comes into the room and shakes my hand. I wonder where that hand was last. Dr. Knopp is a short bulky man with a large head, and he has square fingers. I would like to scoop out his honest eyes and take them home with me. They would look great inside the grape jelly jars in my cellar.

The doctor and I go through our yearly ritual. He looks inside all my facial orifices, and listens to my heart and lungs. I ask him if he's continuing to enjoy life. After the small talk, he checks my testicles, and I try to perceive if he's impressed. He does not appear so inclined, and I remind myself to cancel the Miracle Grow soak after my showers.

Finally comes the one procedure I always dread, the rectal exam to check my prostate. There may be a technical problem with his square fingers and my round hole. I express my concern about this, but Dr. Knopp chuckles and proceeds anyway.

He tells me to bend over and place my elbows on the exam table like some kind of freak. It feels like a medium sized ferret has entered my rectum, and it seems to take the good doctor an exquisitely long time to finish the examination. By the time he's done, I have a white knuckle grip on the exam table, and a bizarre urge to give him my phone number.

After Dr. Knopp has completed the brutal exam, I ask him for the glove, and he slips it into a bio hazard bag before handing it to me. He knows from previous visits not to ask me any questions. It's like when you join the Knights of Columbus.

I hand the nurse my co-pay, while clutching desperately to the last of my dignity. Where the bio hazard bag ended up is personal.

Wednesday

The commercial on the television mentions about a fertility clinic offering $3,500 for eggs. Why wasn't this shit available when Mary was fertile? We could have been retired by now, and living in a warm state. I turn off the set, it's making me feel depressed.

Shuffling into the kitchen, I remove 18 eggs from the refrigerator. The 18 packs are bigger than the 12, just like my penis is bigger than my brothers. Ralph was never able to compensate for this.

I take the eggs outside, leaving the carton on the deck railing, while obtaining the ladder from the shed. Placing the ladder against the side of the house, I carefully climb up onto the roof with the crate of eggs tucked under my arm. My plan is to roll the eggs off of the roof.

The view is breathtaking from my rooftop, and it

makes me feel close to God. There's a dead possum across the street, and its intestines are stretched out at an angle from its body. It reminds me of a business meeting I attended in West Virginia a few years ago. I weep with concern for the baby possums alone in the woods, waiting for a parent who will never return home. The babies will probably need some type of therapy.

When we were children, my brother and I always waited eagerly for our dad to arrive home from work. Most of the time, I was praying he would be delivered in a box. One time while waiting for good old dad, I shit inside his favorite boots. It seemed like a good idea at the time, like putting ice cream in the scotch.

Laughter rolled from me as I placed the shit filled boots in dad's closet. You could not have found a more fun loving and adventurous child than me, but it's funny how time changes things. Later in the evening my merriment died. Extension cords can really damage your shoulders, but they leave remarkable scars. Mary was really impressed when she saw them on our first date.

Reminiscing can be diverting, but I need to get back to the business at hand. I stomp my foot three times on the roof in order to wake up my wife.

I roll 10 eggs off the left side of the roof, and 8 eggs down the right side. Life is a balancing act, and I try to maintain mine. Rolling the eggs from the roof every 6 weeks provides the ant's with a food source, and keeps them from entering the house. Ant spray is expensive, while eggs remain fairly cheap.

My roof is metal, which means it heats up in the summer. Through self experimentation, I have learned that ejaculating onto the hot roof sounds very similar to eggs frying.

Climbing down off the roof, I return the ladder to the shed and go inside the house. Mary is awake, and has managed to ambulate to the kitchen where she's sitting upright at the table.

The ambien must be wearing off, but she still appears

exhausted. I consider taking advantage of her while she's still under the influence of the medication, but there's enough light in her eyes to suggest it would not be a good idea. Instead, I ask what she's planning to have for breakfast. She mumbles something about eggs.

Something tells me, there may be a problem.

Thursday

Stop, drop, and roll will not work in Hell. On my way home from the store this morning, I saw this statement written on a church sign. The pastor who came up with the slogan has my admiration.

The snake is in my belly and the dog is in my bones, but still the sign made me smile. It's good to know your destination, but there was nothing to grin about when I arrived home and turned on the news.

CNN reported about the controversial sentencing of a fifty year old man who had repeatedly raped a twelve year old girl. For some reason this story reminded me of Uncle Percy.

The old man was found guilty at his trial, and the sentence handed down was probation. The light sentence was shocking to some people, including me.

After the sentencing, the judge announced she did not want to send the rapist to prison because of his height. The fifty-year-old man is 5' 1". This is one more reason for me not to like short people or judges, but the wee folk can be great fun at parties.

The judge further explained, she was afraid the old man would become a victim in prison due to his lack of a sufficient altitude. So what. Justice can prevail in many forms, but apparently not in a courthouse.

I'm the embodiment of fairness, but this judge does not have a clue as to what the fuck she's talking about. To make the judge happy they should build a prison just for short people, and call it Shorticca. All the short prisoners could victimize the midgets.

It causes me to wonder how the judge got appointed to her job, most likely the same way as the executives at Enron. The judge's logic is very troubling. The man might be too short to ride the roller coaster at Disney World, but he can rape a child and not go to prison. This makes no kind of sense even to an unreasonable person like me. What a great justice system we have.

Prisons were made for people like this rapist, in the same way mustard was invented for corned beef. The judge should have released the man into the custody of the girl's parents. That would have been a logical and fair sentence. How can you measure justice? I can measure my dick with a yardstick, but how do you measure justice?

Perhaps the judge's concern could be alleviated if we stretched the rapist to make him taller. You can discern when a bird has been squeezed enough by the tremors vibrating through your hand. This thought makes me want to give the rapist a big hug.

Justice is a rarity in today's world, and so is the Pope's semen. Stop, drop, and roll will not work in Hell.

Friday

Today at work, a patient told me how he had attempted to commit suicide by jumping off a bridge. While listening to his story, I was unable to understand what made it so difficult. The only thing you are responsible for is finding a bridge. How exacting can that be? It's like my cat's asshole, you don't often see it, but it's not hard to find.

You could walk into any library and find out where the bridges in town are. This does not seem like an arduous undertaking, any moron should be able to accomplish this.

You do need to make sure the bridge is high enough that death is assured. Becoming a cripple does not count as a successful suicide, and it places an unintended additional burden on society.

The next question you would have to ask yourself, is what type of bridge span should you choose. Do you need to jump off the railing or can you dive? Should you notify a local television station ahead of time to film your jump? Should you be concerned about the mess you are going to make? Maybe killing yourself by leaping off a bridge is more complicated than I first thought.

Is it proper to jump without leaving a note? After finding an appropriate bridge, you need to decide how to climb it. Suicide takes some effort, not much, but some. You could take a cab to the bridge, but somehow this seems lazy, and you should not involve other people in your choice to die.

It's not necessary to jump after you arrive at the perfect departure point, you can just topple over the railing. Any idiot should be able to accomplish this.

I asked the patient if he felt like a failure after the disappointing attempt. Let's face it, if you can't kill yourself then what the fuck can you do. When you kill another person, you have to track them down first. Killing yourself is easy, you are not going anywhere.

Being a self proclaimed suicidal planner, I explained to the patient how everybody needs a plan, just like your 401K. The patient seemed disturbed, and became agitated.

I gave the patient directions to the GWB, and wished him bon voyage.

Monday

Either I have a hearing problem, or the voices in my head are mumbling. The pharmacist is giving me a look that says this situation could turn bad very quickly. His eyes remind me of my mom's before she had cancer. Cancer takes the light from your eyes, and sucks all the life from you, just like a mother-in-law. Cancer has killed off a few members of my family, leaving the odds in my favor.

The pharmacist hands me my prescription while continuing to stare. After making sure my pants are zipped, I proceed to my car and count the pills. This time there are thirty.

The voices who live behind my eyes are whispering softly, like cows thighs rubbing together. Swish, calling my name, swish. Cows inhabit the field across the street from my home, and I have learned over the years to monitor their movements.

You should never look a cow in the eye, they are disturbed animals. They might move slowly, but they are determined beasts, and you can't impede determination.

My intention this morning was to make a quick stop at the pharmacy and be on my way to work, but here I am sitting in the CVS parking lot. I'm going to be late for work, which has been happening far to often lately.

My excessive tardiness could lead to termination, but my job is discomforting, and there's no need to rush headlong into suffering. There are people who believe we deserve to suffer in this life, but I bet they were never accosted by a priest with a bent penis.

When the day finally arrives that my boss decides to fire me, it will liberate me to achieve my calling. I have started to hate my job over the last few years. If everybody at work died, it wouldn't be a bad place to be employed. It's just a game of numbers to a mass murderer. Death was my favorite subject in school even though it was not required.

My mom died many years ago when she caught cancer, not like a cold or a fish. Cancer can smell like hot cross buns, and near the end it gets sticky. I pick at the pimple on my right arm during the drive to work.

The voices in my head have gone silent, but when the wind blows, the hairs in my ears sing.

They need to update the song list.

Wednesday

Wilbert is a nice man to have as a neighbor, but he looks like Donald Rumsfeld, who is not one of my favorite people. My neighbor is puttering around with some old lawnmowers near his garage. He starts trembling as I stride across the yard toward him. Over the years, I have become aware that he may suffer from some type of affliction. I attempt to exhibit some concern for my fellow man.

I ask Wilbert when he plans on bringing the troops home, and a befuddled look crosses his face. Maybe this guy really is Rumsfeld. Most of the citizens in this small town wear the same confused expression, and the majority of them voted for George Bush. My town is like a slow child, you just want to put it to sleep.

My neighbor is acting like he didn't hear me, so I try the question again in Spanish. He begins backing away from me, as tears form in the corners of his eyes.

In order to ease the acid burning in my stomach, I pull up a clump of grass and chew it. The fire in my belly abates long enough for me to smile at Wilbert with my green teeth.

My neighbor quickly retreats inside his house. He's a bizarre man who bears watching. This is a peaceful neighborhood where the police never get called, and I want to keep it that way. Should I knock on his door? My skin itches, and I wish there was a razor in my pocket.

The day will come when I will scoop out Wilbert's eyes and eat them. As age has ravaged my body, the eyesight I possessed as a young man is declining. Perhaps ingesting my neighbor's eyes would help. I will remind him to fill out his organ donor card.

With my boot, I scratch a straight line in the dirt where our properties join. If Wilbert crosses the line today, he will be taken on a one time tour through my cellar. If the rain washes the line away, he will live to see another day. It's in God's hands.

Finding my hands conveniently inside my pockets, I gently scratch my testicles. There are a few grains of sand in the pockets, but no glass.

As soon as I get inside the house, my cat is howling like an injured child. She hasn't been looking too healthy lately. She's starting to remind me of the skinny lady in medical records at work. Scooter is quite old, and there's nothing left of her but skin and bones. Mostly bones. It helps if you squint when looking at her.

She's starting to smell like my grandmother did before she died. Scooter kind of looks like my grandma when the sun hits her whiskers just right.

I'm starting to get hungry, so I slice up some tomatoes on the counter. The way the sharp knife rolls across the tomato skin just before it splits open to let the juice out always excites me. The skin of a tomato, and the skin of a human are not much different.

Scooter is howling again, I pinch her ear and she runs away. She can't really run anymore, it's turned into an antiquated shuffle. I squeeze my own ear and scream. Scooter looks back in my direction, but can't see me because she's blind. Does that make me invisible? A man and his kitty have a unique bond.

After licking the juice off the knife, I throw the tomatoes away and make myself a bologna sandwich.

I can't eat tomatoes, they give me heartburn.

Saturday

When using aluminum foil, always make sure its heavy duty, like magnum condoms.

For many years, I have placed foil in the bottoms of my shoes. The material is refractory, and it protects me from pollution. It's difficult to get your feet inside the shoes without wrinkling the foil, but nothing ventured, nothing gained. It's like sticking a knife in the toaster to pry out your bagel.

Sometimes, I will glue the foil onto the bottoms of my socks. Ingenuity is my middle name, I should have worked for FEMA.

Mary and I are going hiking today, despite the fact she's not Caucasian. Hiking is one of my favorite activities, but my wife has never expressed her feelings on the subject. Generally, you don't see too many black people wandering around in the woods doing what we white folks affectionately call hiking.

While backpacking over the last ten months, I have not encountered a single black person other than Mary, and this causes me to wonder if my wife is unusual. The white people we meet along the trail seem to be friendly, but a bit odd looking.

Maybe I can convince Mary's sister to join us on our next excursion, but after the incident at the stock car races it's not likely.

Hiking in the woods allows you to relax and think clearly without distraction. It's also considered very good exercise, like pulling on a cat's tail.

The drive through the Adirondacks is pretty damn boring even for an environmentalist. By the time we arrive at the trail head, it feels like I swallowed a handful of valium. Removing the knife from underneath my seat wakes me up enough to notice Mary watching me from the corner of her eye. What's her problem?

The knife is for comfort purposes only, I would never injure an animal. For safety reasons you should always carry a weapon in case you run into the previously mentioned odd folks on the trail.

The trail we are exploring is not very wide, but its well defined, like my wife's breasts. I remove the metal trail markers from the trees after we pass by, and toss them into the woods. A true hiker does not need to be on a predetermined path.

Dashing quickly behind a tree, I squat on my haunches, and pretend Mary is hiding from me. It must be great fun to have me as a husband.

My wife encourages me to get back onto the trail, and stop my nonsense. I love my wife, but it's my choice whether or not to obey her. We have been married for 28 years, almost as long as Charlie Manson has been in prison.

A chipmunk skitters across the trail in front of me, reviving memories of Mary's dance instructor. Animals have fur, but they don't have a clothing line, and it causes me to ponder if they are ever embarrassed. What if the little chipmunk is aroused at the sight of a female? He has no trousers to hide his erection, and this does not sit well with my sense of decorum.

My bladder is urging me for release, as I step behind a large tree and let it go. Mary is jealous of my ability to do this even though I have explained to her many times how God favors men.

There aren't any clowns in the woods, which allows me the time to cover my urine with pine needles. Is someone burning cheese nearby?

Mary is waiting patiently beside the trail for me to reappear. I consider warning her about snakes, but we could use a little excitement on this hike. She's a good wife, but I have never had another to compare her with.

I know exactly how many times my sperm has been deposited inside of her over our 28-year marriage, but we are not Catholics. There's a tally kept in my egg notebook on the kitchen counter at home.

I suggest we could run into the bushes and add to the number. Mary laughs, and continues walking. I love her smile a great deal, that's why I keep extra teeth stored in the cellar.

There's a large boulder at the bend of the trail where we take a break, eat some crackers, and drink some water. As we sit on the rock, I realize these are the first crackers we have seen today.

I use the rest period to catch up on my journal, as Mary admires the mountain view. I lick behind her ear until she tells me to stop. I explain how there was not enough salt on the crackers, but she doesn't believe me.

We hike back to the car, and without Mary noticing, I slide the knife back under my seat.

Monday

Going to work is similar to thinking you don't have cancer, and then finding out you do. Today I'm not working, it's remission.

It's a beautiful day to drive into Saratoga, and walk in the park. Mary is working today, which means I will be walking by myself. I'm never really alone, God is with me. He constantly whispers inside my head, and I can only hope, He doesn't peek in the corners.

Congress Park is very small, and right in the center of downtown Saratoga. My cat's ass is small, and it's located in the center of her cheeks. Comparisons can be advantageous, and they allow you to keep things in perspective. It's like looking in the mirror without recognizing the person staring back.

The park is overflowing with a multitude of human- ity, and it makes me nervous even though I'm naturally gregarious. Surveying the park carefully, I fail to detect anyone with loaves or fishes. Does anybody in the park understand about fire regulations? Where are the exit signs located?

There are ducks wandering throughout Congress Park, and you are permitted to feed them if you are so inclined. Before leaving the house this morning, I tucked a pear inside my pocket.

I inspect one of the park benches for urine, and it ap- pears dry, so I take a seat. After chomping a big hunk out of my pear, I examine the bite marks. If the impression is symmetrical, the ducks will receive the remainder of the fruit. The bite mark seems out of alignment which means there's no free lunch. I kick the birds until they vacate my area. Ducks can make a great deal of noise, much like the last person invited to my cellar.

After finishing my snack, I slide the knife out from my boot and hollow out a small hole next to the bench. I bury the pear core, and tap the dirt down with my palm. If nothing else, I'm always fastidious. There's a special feeling you get from burying things, but unfortunately pears can't scream.

While strolling out of the park, I notice three ducks waddling ahead of me. The lead bird wanders into the street, and is struck by a car. The driver does not stop, which forces me to quickly memorize the plate number in order to insure justice is served. Perhaps, later tonight.

The two companion ducks assist the injured bird across the street by pulling at him with their bills and goosing him along. The action seems undignified to me, but then again never leave a duck behind. Semper Fi.

The trio of ducks manages to evade traffic, and make it across the street where they huddle together beside a building. I make my way over to join them out of curiosity, not because my vision is inadequate. Is it better to wear bifocals or be bipolar?

The two chaperon birds cluster around their injured buddy as if they are waiting for something. My purpose in life is to be a helper of others. I place my boot directly over the crippled ducks neck, and press down until somebody snaps their fingers.

The two living ducks look at their companion, and then raise their heads to worship me. After giving them a brief lecture on the futility of helping others, I walk to my car.

Tuesday

Why does my shadow follow me? Am I acting suspicious? This day had an unusual start when Mary found a hair inside her English Muffin. I prefer hair around my muffins, but not in them.

Why do they call them English muffins when they are manufactured in New Jersey? Most of the residents of New Jersey don't speak English, but the state does have an abundance of prisons. I wonder if that's where they make the muffins.

I became a prison pen pal in order to encourage those behind bars. It's also useful to make connections in case you ever need a favor. The last letter I mailed was written in braille, and as of today there has been no response. Convicts can be sullen.

Some states use convicts as cheap labor in order to repair their highways. Some might consider this another form of slavery, but I prefer to consider it time well spent.

The law allows prisoners to be used as laborers in many states. If they can work for the state while serving time, why can't they have a state job after their release? Could it be due to the fact, the state would have to pay them more than thirty cents a day?

Grocery stores are one of the few places that will hire convicted felons, and the next time you decide to scream at the shelf replenisher it might be an excellent idea to remember the fact.

My grocery store claims to stay open 24 hours. What the fuck does that mean? After 24 hours, do they close? Life can be confusing. I search for an answer by consulting the lines on my palm. There are no hairs on my palm, unlike my wife's muffin.

Now my shadow has dreadlocks, and it makes me wish Bob Marley was alive to see this.

Wednesday

Why do people wave at me when I'm driving? It's very distracting, and it seems to happen more when I'm cruising on country roads. Are country people more friendly? They don't know how to make good ice cream, but they exhibit great dexterity when milking a cow.

Sometimes it's a pleasure to have people wave at me, but I seldom return the wave. I expect people to acknowledge me. It would be honorable to run over the people who don't wave, but concern over the damage it would cause my car keeps me from doing this. Auto repair costs are extremely high. My wife considers me frugal.

Where did the wave originate? Did Cain wave at Abel? Did Adam wave to Eve? I have noticed how Caucasian people seem to wave in an awkward fashion. It could be caused by the polo shirts.

Is it rude to wave at a blind man? Am I required to return a wave if my shoulder hurts, or is a nod of the head permissible? Can the meaning of a wave be misconstrued? Will despondent people flock to me if I provide them with a wave? When I wave at a person with no arms, how do they respond? How long should you maintain a wave before it's polite to cease? It's too bad mom's not here to answer my questions.

People often die before you can ask them for forgiveness, although at that juncture it may be pointless. Waving at dead people will get you arrested in some southern states.

Does the President ever wave at strangers? George Bush is suddenly concerned about immigration, and I wonder if he would be angry to see me wave at a Mexican. Why are Mexicans the only immigrants the President seems concerned about? My only concern is trying to figure out what that shit is inside a burrito.

The truth of the matter is Caucasian people are afraid to be outnumbered in this country, but it's inevitable, like hair growing out of your ear. Don't be afraid white people, you can wave and make a friend. Give and it shall be given unto you.

All this week they have been showing the immigration protest marches on television. I waved at the masses of people even though they could not see me. CNN had coverage all day long, and my arm got a little tired. It was gratifying to have the news focus on something other than a missing white woman.

In my neighborhood, waving with a knife in your hand receives more scrutiny.

Thursday

Thank God for the discovery of psychiatry. It makes me wonder how people ever managed to deal with their problems before antidepressants and the voodoo theories of psychobabble. After meeting with my psychiatrist today, I realized they simply don't know what the fuck they are talking about.

I always believed when I got pissed off and yelled at people it was simply because they made me angry. According to my psychiatrist nothing can be that easily explained. He informed me, I have Intermittent Explosive Disorder, and the best news is, it's not my fault.

It makes me ecstatic to be diagnosed with a disease that permits me to go out and kill people, and remain - blameless. It's not my fault, I have Intermittent Explosive Disorder. Thank you psychiatry for eradicating all of my responsibility, and enabling me to feel good about the exceptional work I do.

They will come up with some type of syndrome next. It always rotates back and forth, syndromes and disorders. There's something here for everybody, and the pharmaceutical companies will make a pill to support your diagnosis.

Some of my capsules come in yummy colors, but since my doctor has tried to poison me, it's too dangerous to ingest them. On every medication label there should be a warning that reads, Use Care When Walking in Blood After Taking This Medication. Psychiatry has the answers for all of the world's problems.

The doctor's may have all the answers, but I'm left

with unanswered questions. Why does the mention of oral competition excite me? Why do worms float in my toilet? How far can you walk if your feet are asleep? What the hell is a significant other? Does my psychiatrist have the answers hidden in a book? The snake is in my belly, and the dog is in my bones. Do they have a medication for that? I doubt it.

Nothing helps me relax like watching the grass in my yard bend in the breeze. Sometimes the wind is difficult to see, but the grass knows it's there.

This afternoon, I noticed some moles were digging up my yard. Using the lawnmower as a mole eradicator enabled me to learn something new. The little creatures have the ability to scream.

I have Intermittent Explosive Disorder, which allows me to bellow right back at them.

Friday

This morning I woke up, but there's a sunrise coming down the road when my eyes will remain closed. Life is an adventure, like eating ice cream at the beach.

I put depilatory cream on my ankles every Friday, so I won't end up like my mother. Hair on your ankles is an abnormality.

A few days ago Mary used an extra button from my shirt to replace a missing button on my pants. That's just not natural, but I wouldn't consider it abnormal. You need to be able to differentiate between the two.

It's almost time for me to pick up Mary from work, and I need to get my shit together. She works at a large hospital in Saratoga that's named after the town. Hospitals can be pleasant places to work, but my experiences as a patient have not been pleasurable. Saratoga Hospital has a hairy armed aide named Paul working on the same unit with Mary. I bring the depilatory cream with me.

During the drive into town, I notice a bike rider on

the crest of the hill ahead of me. Why are they always at a spot on the hill where you can't see if traffic is coming the other way?

I should pass the rider, but fear causes me to hesitate, just like when Father Francis came into the cabins at camp. Life is a circle.

Pulling up alongside the cyclist, I nudge him gently with the car bumper. Have I gone blind? I only masturbated twice today, but the rear view mirror reveals the bike rider has disappeared. Maybe he was a magician.

I pull over on the shoulder of the road to investigate the illusion. This is turning out to be a fun day. Walking carefully along the edge of the road, I notice a bike in the ditch and a man lying next to it. It's possible the man has traveled a long distance causing him to be exhausted, but he should have found a hotel instead of resting in the ditch.

Climbing down into the gully is no easy task, and I'm concerned about injuring myself. I make it safely to the bottom without falling, but somehow one shoe got scuffed. This makes me angry enough to kick the rider twice. Technically he's no longer a rider, now he's a sleeper. Could he be a terrorist cell member?

My kicks have not received any response from the man. After pulling down his socks, I check his ankles and apply a small amount of the depilatory cream. I consider leaving my phone number in case the man wants to thank me after he wakes up, but my number is unlisted.

Taking a wrench from my pocket, I tap the man lightly behind his ear, this poor guy is really tired. I wander over to the bike and leave him to rest.

Using the wrench, I remove the tires from the bike, and tote them back to my car. The smell of rubber will permeate the vehicle after a few days in the trunk.

It's getting late, and Mary will be wondering what's taking me so long. I leave the sleeping man to his business, and drive to the hospital. My wife is happy to see me in spite of my late arrival.

On the drive home, we notice two police cars and an

ambulance parked alongside the road. I smile at the policeman as he waves us by. Mary's eyes have questions, but she doesn't ask.

I can almost smell the rubber.

Saturday

This is some scary shit. I'm walking down the hallway in my home and can't remember why. This type of thing has been happening a lot lately. Sometimes, I can remember my destination, and other times my direction indicator shuts off.

I could have been diagnosed with a brain lesion, and forgot it's there. This temporary loss of memory could turn out to be fun, or a good excuse to do something really bad. It's possible that I won the lottery and can't remember.

My bladder is pressuring me to take a piss. After finishing up, I shake off my dick and wash my hands. Cleanliness is next to Godliness, but I can't remember how to recite the prayer. Some pervert is inside the mirror gawking at me, and I try to stare him down, but this guy is unshakable.

The phone is ringing in the kitchen, so I cautiously slip out of the bathroom, never taking my eyes off the stranger in the mirror. Generally, I prefer to screen my calls, but I reach the phone just before the answering machine kicks in. My doctor screens my prostate, and there are screens on all my windows. I answer the phone in order to avoid confusion.

Steve is on the line from Harry and David, and he wants to sell me some cheesecake. Cheesecake is one of my favorite indulgences, but before agreeing to buy anything, I request to speak with Harry or David. Steve informs me they are unavailable, but claims he is fully capable of handling my order.

This guy Steve must think he's talking to a fucking idiot. I demand to know what kind of business Harry and

David are running, if they can't take the time to speak with a customer. Steve begins to apologize, but I cut the moron short. I tell him if they changed the name to Harry and Steve or Steve and David, it would then be logical for someone named Steve to call me.

After my constructive comments, Steve is no longer responding and I detect a dial tone. We must have been disconnected, but it didn't seem like we were bonding anyway.

Wandering down the hallway to our bedroom, I re-move one of my socks and stick it under Mary's pillow. It will be interesting to see if I can remember it's there.

Sunday

The Saratoga Deli is where I shop for cheese. The rusty machine in my cellar allows me to carve all my meat at home. Stepping up to the counter, I request one pound of white american cheese, and it makes me sound like a racist.

The clerk begins slicing my cheese, and after each sliver drops onto the paper, I caress myself. Rhythm is everything, and it seems like we are working toward a satisfying conclusion.

The clerk abruptly ceases slicing in order to quiz a mother about whether her child would like to sample a slice of cheese. The mother nods her head affirmatively, accepts a slice of my cheese, and passes it to her child sitting in the grocery cart.

When I shop tomorrow, my groceries will be sitting in the same spot where her kid is now shitting in the basket. This situation leaves me stunned without my hammer. My eyes shift from the clerk to the mother as I wait for judge-ment to fall.

I'm as magnanimous as the next guy, but that was my fucking slice of cheese, and nobody asked my permission to make a donation. I'm not wearing my Feed the Children T-shirt. Nobody is paying any attention to me, it's like sitting in a meeting with ten nurses at work.

I snatch the cheese away from the brat, and he begins to wail like an imprisoned priest. I love children, but not when they steal from innocent people.

The mother screams, and demands to know what the hell is going on. It usually takes women longer to become aware of danger. I slowly explain to her about how the repo man recovers his cheese. This whole situation helps me understand how the Palestinians feel.

The child is now screaming at the top of his lungs with great gusto. It makes me wish I had a sock, or better yet a claw hammer. It's rewarding to see that the child is showing a little remorse for stealing.

A crowd has gathered, and there are too many eyes watching me. Grabbing my pound of cheese from the counter, I run toward the checkout area.

The girl at the register does not attempt to pilfer a slice of my cheese, which reassures me the world is back in balance.

Upon arriving home, I weigh the cheese to ascertain it's an unequivocal pound.

Monday

There are seven days in a week, and there are seven knives hidden inside my car. One under each of the front seats, one in the pocket of each front door, one in the pocket of each rear door, and one in the glove box. Life is all about order and perfection. Thinking of all that cold steel in close proximity makes me want to push someone in front of a train.

Today is my day off, but I need to take Mary to work. She's only allowed to drive on special occasions, and this is not one of them. She's a proud employee of Saratoga Hospital, and keeping the beds full is how I do my part.

I drop my wife off in front of the Emergency entrance, even though going to work is not an emergency. It makes me feel guilty, but my guilt does not linger, it disappears instantly like flushing a toilet.

After pulling out of the parking lot, I stop for the red light at the corner. As an ex convict you learn to watch your step. There's a compact blue car almost touching my rear bumper, making me believe the driver is farsighted.

When the light turns green, I observe the little car in my rear view mirror while keeping my foot on the brake. A middle-aged woman is behind the wheel, and she begins beeping her horn. This could be entertaining. I honk my horn back at her, and she appears to be getting agitated. Removing the knife from under the drivers seat, I lick the blade to make it slide easier.

Opening my door, I proceed cautiously back toward her car. You should always be careful when approaching strangers in case they are dangerous.

The woman is screaming profanities at me, causing me to wonder what has made her day go all wrong. Using all my strength, I plunge the knife through the roof of her car just above her head. I gently caress her brunette curls with my left hand, as I hold out my right hand to introduce myself. She screams, and I smile. If you have an outgoing personality, it's not difficult to make friends.

The woman throws her car into reverse, and backs away with tires squealing. What has happened to this world? Can't anybody be polite anymore? Tires continue to screech as she rounds the corner without even saying goodbye.

Getting into my car, I proceed home after stopping along the way to buy two dozen donuts. They are not for me, but I have a sneaky feeling the police might be coming to visit. Donuts keep them happy.

After arriving home, I place the donuts on the deck railing as my early warning system.

I will have to remember to stop at the hardware store tomorrow and replace the knife.

Tuesday

Eating breakfast is a sign of weakness, and inconsistency is one of the things the Grim Reaper looks for. So far in my life, I have managed to maintain a good relationship with the Death Master by referring a large volume of business his way.

This morning, I may have to make an exception to my rule. The lawn needs to be mowed, but you should never touch the grass without eating first. It's proper etiquette.

I pour myself a heaping bowl of raisin bran, there's only so much fiber you can get from eating carpet. Measuring out a half cup of skim milk, I slowly pour it over the top of the cereal. If allowed to bubble, the milk will leak damaging compounds into the air.

Milk is a dangerous substance, and it can cause cancer in humans. My mom whispered that information in my ear just before she died, and then she tried to stick her finger in my eye.

The milk on my raisin bran has the appearance of watered down semen. I glance out the window while waiting for the milk to settle. The grass is waving to me, like a child to its father.

As my gaze returns to the cereal, a fly has crash landed in my bowl, and is struggling to escape. Should I attempt to rescue the fly? Am I prepared to do CPR? What about rescue breathing? I'm afraid it's bad news for the fly.

Picking up my spoon, I use it to press the fly underneath the milk. When I lift the spoon, the nasty insect floats to the surface and weakly kicks it's leg. Memories of my brother flood through my mind. There was a time when I held Ralph underwater, but he put up a better fight than the fly seems capable of doing.

Once more I push the fly below the milk, and this time when the spoon is released, the insect drifts to the surface and remains motionless. It looks like we have a floater.

Scooter is awake, and she wanders into the kitchen to greet me. My kitty is old and dying, but she still gets hungry. I have a special breakfast for her, even better than Denny's.

Scooter's health has taken a turn for the worse over the last few months. When she pees there are blood clots in her urine. I buy the green litter to remind me of Christmas.

I scoop the fly into my spoon along with some milk, and tap the floor with my foot. Scooter follows the vibration from the tapping to stand in front of me. As she looks up in my direction, it permits me to see my face reflected in her blind eyes. I hold the spoon full of milk and fly in front of her nose, and she laps it up. She's a good kitty. Scooter looks up expectantly for seconds, but there are no more flies.

I pinch her ear, which causes her to howl and run away. The howling does not irritate my kitty, she has gone deaf also. Old age can be unpleasant, but Scooter does not play pinball.

I place the remaining raisin bran in the refrigerator, so it can be used to make muffins. Mary will be proud of me.

Before going outside to mow the lawn, I put in my ear plugs in order to muffle the screams.

Thursday

Fall is the perfect time to buy apples in New York state, they are cheap. I don't use the apples for eating, but peeling is good practice. After rubbing the peels on my stomach and tossing the skins into the garbage, the peeled apples are placed in a bowl on the kitchen counter. Many years ago, I used to rub the peels on my chest, but it moved.

I place a dozen apples that haven't been peeled off to the side, and stick one Band-Aid on each of them. We don't want any serious injuries today.

Cows live across the street from my house, and they roam around pretty much as they please. Nobody pushes them around. Sometimes they come close to the wire fence surrounding the large field, and this allows me to watch them from my window with binoculars. Most of the cows drool like Aunt Amy after her stroke.

Cows are dangerous animals, and need to be kept under close surveillance. They may seem harmless and slow, but they are methodical.

Dumping the dozen apples with Band-aids into a bag, I carry them across the street. Most of the cows ignore me, but I sense they are aware of my every move. How could they miss anything with those huge eyes? If only I could get close enough to lick one of their eyeballs.

Several of the bovines are walking across the field in my direction. Actually, they are ambling. I toss one Band-aid wrapped apple at the nearest cow. Thunk! The apple smacks the beast in the side, and it sounds like a talking drum. I throw another, this time hitting a different animal in the face. Its eye starts to swell, and suddenly the cow looks oriental. In order to satisfy my urge to understand animal behavior, I toss the remainder of the apples in the general direction of the herd.

The cows slowly wander away from me toward the opposite side of the field. Their movements impress me as they maintain good group discipline, but their ability to dodge apples is not extraordinary. They should try dodging baseballs while tied to a tree.

When I was a teenager, my dad spent an hour throwing baseballs at me after roping me to a tree. Dad had a nasty curve ball, and I could never figure out which way it was going to break. Memories of dad cause my stomach to burn, but drinking milk will alleviate the pain.

I wave at the cows, but they aren't coordinated enough to return my greeting. It makes me want to climb over the fence and kick some udder.

The cows are huddled together on the far side of the field. They show no emotion, but you can be sure they are plotting revenge. Cows are quiet, and they can sneak up on you.

I run across the street to the safety of my house,

without turning my back on the animals.

Mary's in the kitchen making apple sauce, and she thanks me for peeling the apples. I moo.

Friday

Would you place your child in close proximity to a tiger's cage in order to take a picture? A mom and dad did exactly that at the County Fair this week. This dumb act encouraged one of the tigers to reach out through the cage, and try to detach the young man's head. Tigers being tigers.

I certainly hope, the parents managed to get a good snapshot. Film can be very expensive.

Apparently the tiger was far sighted, which caused the animal to miss its mark. The big cat did manage to get one claw on the young man's head, but that's like having one number in the lotto. You get nothing. The child received fourteen stitches, and the scare of his young life. They should have fed the irresponsible parents to the tiger.

After the incident, people began protesting and complaining about whether it was necessary to have these types of cats at a County Fair. They should be bellyaching about the dumb ass parents who would place their child in such danger.

There's a very good reason why they need the jungle cats at the County Fair. In this town, the only reason a fat redneck would ever leave his stool at the bar is so he could stagger over to the Fair and gawk at the tigers. The cats help in the fight against alcoholism. They have cows at the Fair, but nobody ever complains about them.

Personally, I have never attended a County Fair, but it's not because the animals frighten me. Fairs are a place where fat sweaty white people like to congregate, similar to a Wal-Mart.

I would like to make a suggestion in order to calm the small town hysteria. The County Fair should be surrounded by a fence twenty feet tall, and after paying the admission fee, patrons would be required to remain on the grounds until the tiger is fed.

During this time, one tiger would be permitted to run loose on the Fairgrounds. This would be explained to potential ticket buyers, giving them one opportunity to change their mind before entering. Everyone deserves a chance in life, including a Jehovah Witness.

Think how exciting it would be to know there's one tiger wandering free, looking for supper. You could attach yourself to a large group of people, cognizant of the fact you only have to outrun one of them. Better yet, just listen for screams of agony, and then hurry to the exhibits in the opposite direction.

You could buy a sausage sandwich, and slip it inside your mother's purse. The County Fair could be fun for the whole family, and good exercise too.

Would you place your child in front of a tiger's cage to take his picture?

Saturday

The news is on, but it's without Huey Lewis. The world is a marketplace, but they don't allow you to touch the melons.

CNN is my favorite news station, the initials are wholesome. Three initials are safe for television news shows, but people with three names are generally untrustworthy. Lee Harvey Oswald, John Wayne Gacy, George Wallace Bush. Enough said.

There's a story on CNN about a grocery worker who arrived at his workplace with two large knives, and proceeded to go crazy. I'm thinking the man was probably nuts long before he ever got to work.

You can't beat a story containing both knives and lunatics. These types of tales always head in a direction I appreciate, like when Mary drives me to Long John Silvers. That's a special occasion.

The grocery worker with the large knives allegedly stabbed eight of his co-workers. This tells me they were not very quick on their feet. CNN is calling it a grocery worker on a rampage. The titles they come up with for these incidents are amusing.

The man's co-workers must have done something to get on his nerves. As I watch the story, it causes me to wonder about the possibility of renting one of these rampagers. Rent a rampager has a nice ring to it.

I would love to lease one, and have him come to my job to fuck up a few people. I wouldn't want any of my co-workers killed, there's no suffering in death, but the thought of having them sliced makes me feel warm inside. Nothing serious, just enough so when they look in a mirror, they will be reminded of me.

I wonder what a rampager would charge as a fee? If I were to provide the weapons, and transportation to and from the site, could I receive a lower rate?

The grocery store where this happened was open for business a few hours later. How did they get the store cleaned up that quick? Were they able to do an adequate job of cleaning the splattered blood off the vegetables? What if they missed a spot, like my boss when she fills out the vacation schedule.

Blood on the floor at work would not be a bad thing, and blood on my sneakers is tolerable if it's for a good cause, but blood on my celery is unacceptable.

CNN is showing tape of the rampager being placed in a police car. He looks familiar.

Monday

It's early morning as I'm driving through Saratoga on my way to work. The streets are nearly empty, but as I pass the cemetery, there's a crowd of people gathered near one of the graves.

Being naturally inquisitive, I stop to see what's going on. The hairs on the side of my neck whisper to me, stop, look, and learn.

Rolling down the window, I suck in a deep breath of the fresh early morning air, and it makes my whole body tingle. Glancing into the rear view mirror, I perceive my tongue lolling out the corner of my mouth. Too much medication this morning? With my left hand, I shove the troublesome organ back inside my mouth. Things in the mirror may appear nearer than they are, but that was too close.

I will never under any circumstances put my right hand close to my face. My right hand is used to hold me when I urinate, and to shake peoples hands. This makes me a functional person.

After vacating my car, I stroll toward the group of people at the edge of the cemetery. A preacher is standing at the head of a grave, and a large cluster of mourners are gathered to his right. Someone must be getting buried, and I wonder if they are dead. I'm not dressed for the occasion, but nobody seems to pay any attention as I proceed closer to the assemblage. My nose is not running, but I'm innocuous.

I position myself behind a woman at the rear of the throng. She has short brown hair, a wide ass, and a long slender neck. After admiring her neck for a few moments, I hang my head, as tears stream down my cheeks. Sometimes my emotions get the best of me. I wonder if anyone else feels like singing.

Wiping the tears on my shirt sleeve, permits me to maintain my dignity. Moving closer to the woman, I breathe softly on the back of her neck, causing her companion to notice me.

Her associate is a gruff looking burly man, who has a flat spot on top of his head. Is he the last of the Mohegan's? The freakish man has grabbed hold of my arm, and is attempting to guide me away from the assembly.

Finding myself enjoying the companionship, I ask his name, and he responds by asking for some identification. Now that's a tough issue, and there's an air of suspicion to his question that does not make me happy. I suggest that he might want to amend the tone of his voice before we have a double decker funeral.

The man's grip on my arm has become somewhat uncomfortable, and I can't remember if there are any aspirins in the car. This guy is really putting pressure on my elbow, which forces me to involuntarily jam my thumb into the little hollow spot below his Adams' apple. My patience has its limits.

The painful squeezing on my arm is immediately relieved, and this allows me to regain my bearings. The annoying man is lying on the ground, and he seems to be in some type of respiratory distress. He should think about cutting back on cigarettes.

I apologize to my new friend for using my right hand, and suggest he might want to apply some antibacterial soap when he arrives home. Some of the other mourners have noticed us, and I ask if anyone knows how to perform the Heimlich maneuver.

Several good Samaritans are running our way, so I leave the gentleman in the care of the rescuers. It's nice to see how quickly folks respond to a person in need.

Before getting into my car, I wipe my right thumb off on the grass.

Tuesday

How long does it take for an elephant to lift its leg? My son spent five weeks in basic training, and then was sent to Afghanistan to fight. We have been training the Iraqi army for almost five years, but still they are not ready. Does this seem like a long basic training to anybody else but me?

Is it possible the Iraqi's don't really want to fight because they have somebody to do their fighting for them? That's what brothers are for, and we are not even related.

There are a great many questions, but very few answers. Why do we fight a war, and yet don't want to injure anyone? Selective targets do not win wars, and lite beer is not really beer.

Every day our troops have to be extremely careful about when to shoot and when to hold their fire, which places them in additional danger. The enemy is not forced to fight with these types of restrictions.

Everyone who resides in the country you are at war with should be considered a target. If they do not desire to be designated as a target, they should evacuate or surrender. If you are not thirsting for a milk shake, don't order your ice cream from a person with Parkinson's.

When our Marines are fired upon, they should be free to fire back without being concerned about court martial's if they happen to hit a civilian. If the enemy is not made to suffer, how can you defeat him? Does anybody remember World War II, which by the way was the last war we won?

Now we want wars without casualties, except for our own. Our own casualties don't seem to matter as much as some poor Iraqi civilian.

My neighbor looks just like the Secretary of Defense, and this allows me to question him about the war. Wilbert has no answers that he's willing to share with me.

When I was in high school, there was a kid named Scully who used to bully me all day long. He would slap the back of my head during class, and trip me in the hallway. After about a week of this nonsense, I got tired, like when Mary put the secobarbital in my soup.

I caught Scully outside his home one evening, and beat his ass down with a wooden baseball bat. Wood is good. I defeated my enemy decisively, and despite not having a victory banner, he never gave me any more problems.

In retrospect, I should have cut his phone lines, disrupted his electrical power, and cut off his supply routes. The next day, I could have repaired all the damage at my expense and baked Scully a cake. That would have shown him.

If the elephant is lifting his leg, you should have ample time to get out from under it.

Friday

Today, they are having fire safety instruction at work. We actually get to practice putting out fires on patients, and this could turn out to be fun. They don't use real patients, the hospital has stand-ins. We cover the fake patients with a sheet to smother the fire. It's like a Klan rally without the burning crosses.

I think the training should be more realistic, like not wearing a condom. Why can't we start a real fire in the building? If a few patients die, they could be known as the designated casualties.

The class instructor is pretending to be a patient in distress. He's an extremely obese man, which means he won't be able to escape. The class is starting, and I don't want to miss anything in case the fat man starts to sizzle.

There should be a law to make corpulent people pay more taxes. When I stroll down the street, it's my desire to use the sidewalk. As a taxpayer it's also my right. When a blimp is coming toward me from the opposite direction, there's not enough room for both of us on the footpath.

Generally, I will step off the sidewalk and allow the lump to pass. I could force the butterball to step aside, but the grass would be damaged.

The tubby fuck's tax burden should be higher if I have to yield my use of the sidewalk. There's an unequal dispersion of space.

You should never daydream in a public arena. Everybody in the class is staring at me, as if expecting something. I check my pant's zipper to be sure the lizard is in its cage. Everything seems to be where it should be, and the world is a safer place.

The enormous instructor is poured into the wheel-chair, and it's my turn to extinguish the fire in his lap. How the fuck did they squeeze his fat ass into the chair? I hope the staff recognizes they are seeing an engineering wonder.

A fellow employee hands me a soot-stained sheet, which I refuse to accept. Why can't I have a clean sheet? My obstinate nature can appear quickly in certain situations. I'm like a one-eyed dog trying to find his bone.

Striding out of the classroom, I head toward the linen closet in the hallway. Everybody will wait for me, or someone will get hurt.

After removing a laundered sheet from the closet, I withdraw the bottle from my pants pocket, and pour a liberal amount of liquid onto the sheet. Now we are cooking.

As soon as I return to the class, the fat man starts a fire on top of the flame resistant pad in his lap, and looks at me expectantly. He probably thinks I ran out and got him a sandwich.

As I run forward with the sheet, I pray he doesn't smell the butane.

Sunday

July 30, 2006. It's a warm sunny day, and I'm breaking my rule about dates and years in this journal. Scooter died today, leaving an empty place in my heart that will never be filled. Maybe a grilled cheese sandwich would help.

Scooter stretched out her old legs, passed gas, and went to be with God. I hope he feeds her well and keeps her litter box clean. She was always sensitive about odors.

Pulling on my wading boots, I look to the sky, and promise Scooter there will be some company coming to join her.

Friday

Mary and I are going to the African American Family Festival today. The admission is free, but you have to pay for the food. The festivities last all day long with music that can make your heart flutter. The revelries continue til dusk, when mounted police come and force the last of the celebrants to evacuate. The snorting horses, and the officer's batons gleaming under the street lights, interfuse with the screams to make an extraordinary musical composition.

I'm not an African, but I can appreciate good music even if it makes me appear awkward. As a Caucasian, my dancing deficiencies will be accentuated today. My wife and I still manage to have a great deal of fun together. My rhythm improves in the bedroom. She tells her relatives, I'm visiting from the group home.

The sun is shining brightly, and it warms the hairless skin on the back of my head. This is the perfect climate for hatching flies, and it makes me thankful that I remembered the sun screen.

The yearly Festival is held in Albany, which is the capital of New York State. Out of all the cities in this state, I have no idea why they choose Albany as the capital. The capital should be representative of the state's condition, and it would have been more appropriate to choose Schenectady. Some of the statues in front of the downtown office buildings are quite impressive, and they are anatomically correct, but otherwise Albany is not memorable.

Finding an available parking space can be a pain in the ass, but I discover one within walking distance of the Festival. As soon as I park, it becomes very obvious to me that the white folks have not turned out in great numbers. This is fortuitous. When the sun is shining brightly, the glare from Caucasian's skin can cause damage to your eyes. You need to be aware of the Surgeon Generals warning.

There are literally hundreds of food booths lining both sides of the outdoor plaza, and the aroma floating in the air is orgasmic. Slobber leaks from the corner of my mouth, and begins trickling down my chin, but I don't wipe it off. There's no need to draw attention to myself. Some of the vendors are selling carved statues and various crafts. There are even a few medical vans offering free check ups.

There's a special redolence to the meats that are being cooked, and I wonder if the chefs might share some of their recipes with me. I purchase an ox tail from one of the vendors, and put it in my pocket for later.

A hollow-eyed black man wearing a white coat approaches, and proceeds to stand directly in front of me. The man is completely blocking my path. People never come close to me voluntarily, making me wonder if the man is unstable. There are no tattoos on my body to forewarn folks, but my eyes are foreboding.

The man asks me about my health, and offers me a free prostate screening. The proposal leaves me speechless. The only other time this happened was when Mary was naked.

After staring at the man, my wife turns her angelic face in my direction. It's almost like she's expecting some reaction from me. Her eyes are sparkling with inner joy, and she has the beginning of a smile on her lips.

Many responses to this man's odd offer go through my mind, but the helpers inside my head narrow them down to two.

The man repeats his pitch, and I attempt to ascertain if this is some kind of joke. My first thought is to explain how I came to the Festival today hoping someone would invite me inside a medical van, and stick their finger up my ass.

With some prompting from my inner guide, I decide it's prudent to go with my second answer. I inform the gentleman that his offer is enticing, but an indescribable injury is about to befall him if he doesn't get the fuck away from me.

The man hustles away, and folds into the crowd. I place the ox tail near the rear bumper of the medical van as a warning to my fellow travelers.

Mary and I continued to roam aimlessly through the plaza in search of my dignity. I glimpsed the prostate man in the crowd several times, but he never came close enough for me to pull his white coat.

The rest of the day turned out to be quite entertaining, even when Mary's throat started to hurt from excessive chuckling.

Monday

I have a job interview scheduled for today, and it's making me nervous. I have killed people without feeling wired like this, I can't understand what the fuck is wrong with me. Before exiting the house, I grab a glass of water and take a couple xanax. Job interviews should be tranquilizing.

After parking outside the huge cardiology building, I scan the lot for any movement that's out of the ordinary. It appears to be a secure environment, but it pays to remain alert, in order to avoid becoming a victim.

Using the rear view mirror as a guide, I strategically place some black pepper on my teeth. This will cause the interviewer to focus on my chompers, and not allow them to notice my eyes. If you want the job, you can never let them observe your eyes.

I'm applying for a position as an EKG technician. The heart is a very familiar organ to me. Hearts are easy to stop, but hard to start, like my old Mercury Tracer.

The cardiology department is located on the third floor which seems completely logical to me. I clutch the railing tightly while climbing the stairs, in order to avoid an accident. I have a fear of falling off stairs, but it's safer than riding in the elevator.

People piss in the corners of elevators, and if the car gets stuck between floors, you will be inhaling stale urine until the rescuers arrive. Odors are particulate, which means you are breathing into your lungs little chunks of whatever you are smelling.

After ascending to the third floor safely, I loosen my belt before going through the door. The police have an easier time catching you if your pants are too tight.

After opening the stairwell door, the first thing I notice is a sign that reads Please Check In. I don't like being told what to do, and am not sure what they mean by checking in. This is not the fucking airport, and nobody can force me to do things. Despite having taken the xanax, anger surges through me like a viagra boner.

A curly haired receptionist is watching me from her cubicle. Somebody used a shotgun to splatter freckles all over her face. One of my sisters had the identical blemishes, but she's dead now.

Annie wants to know if she can help me, and I find her pleasant attitude refreshing. It's not likely she can help, but I inform her about my appointment with Janet Wilson for an interview. She instructs me to have a seat, while apprising me that Janet will be right with me.

I prefer to stand with my back against the wall, so nobody can creep up on me. Seats are for losers, unless you are tired.

My name is being called, and I wonder if they spelled it right. Glancing up at the ceiling, I'm unable to perceive any cameras, but the hairs on my thighs are signaling to my brain that someone's watching.

My name is called again, and it appears to be resonating from the short rotund woman standing across the room. Is this the idiot who keeps calling my name? She reminds me of Aunt Lily after she started taking the depakote. Listening to a few voices is better than a massive weight gain.

I casually stroll toward her while maintaining eye contact. She holds out a pasty hand, and introduces herself as Janet Wilson. I demand that she provide me with two forms of identification, but she simply smiles and shakes my hand. I grin back, and wonder if she can imagine where my hand was last.

As she guides me down the hallway to her office, Janet seems unable to remove her gaze from my teeth. Before she can offer me a seat, I plop into one of the uncomfortable stiff-backed chairs. She needs to be made aware of my unpredictability.

She wants to know what my responsibilities are at my present job, but before answering, I lick the backs of my hands and place them palms down on top of her desk. Her face is reflected in my saliva, and she has the eyes of a swine. This leads me to conclude she's not a Muslim.

I respond to her question by explaining how I have worked all my life. She wants me to be more specific about my job duties, but I inform her that due to confidentiality laws they do not allow me to disclose that information.

Janet is beginning to look uncomfortable, like Mary did this morning when I asked her to roll over. That's why I never enter strange people's homes, but I will park in their driveways.

I walk one of my hands like a spider across Janet's desk, as she rambles on about what a fast paced environment I will be working in if they decide to hire me. It doesn't appear she has been moving at a fast pace lately.

I scratch my nuts, and instantaneously place my hands back on top of her desk. How's that for fast paced? She doesn't seem to have noticed me, and I make a note of her observation flaws.

Janet questions me about taking a tour of the facility, but I'm forced to decline. All my shows are local. Her porker eyes are twitching, and it reminds me of a former Nurse Manager who had the same problem.

I untie my shoes, and stick a finger in my ear, as Janet makes a request for references. I write down a few names and pass them across her desk. She informs me, the Personnel Department will be in touch as she escorts me to the stairwell.

Sometimes potential employers will ask why my references have numbers after their names that are not associated with phones, but Janet doesn't ask.

She does suggest, I should be careful going down the stairs because my shoes are untied. It will be delightful to have a boss who cares about me.

Tuesday

Standing on my front deck, I meditate on the mysteries of life while watching crows wander through my yard. I wonder if there's a special place for crows to go before they die. Have you ever seen a bird drop out of the sky? When crows die of old age, they must be on the ground. What about the baby boomers? If thousands of crows die each day, why aren't they dropping from the sky? Fuck the cats and dogs, it should be raining crows.

Do the young crows take the old birds to a place where they wait for death? Do they force them to stay there, and not allow them to fly? Could there be a retirement home for the birds in Wisconsin?

Not a day goes by without large numbers of crows coming to sit in my yard. Most of the birds could use a trip to Weight Watchers, the excess weight puts a limit on their flying hours. The crows have shiny black eyes, but I have never been able to get close enough to see if they blink.

The birds don't seem to comprehend, I would never cause them any harm. My fifth grade teacher was the same way, but I know where he went to die.

I have no desire to injure the birds, but there are questions which need to be answered. When I toss a stone at one of the birds, it leaps high into the air, causing me to miss. Crows have extremely strong thighs.

Running inside the house, I grab Mary's shotgun from the closet, and I'm pleased to find she forgot to unload it.

Life should be tidy, like a toilet, which leaves me free to eradicate the worlds confusing elements.

While firing the shotgun, I receive the answer to my primary question. Crows go to die in my yard.

Wednesday

Insignificance is just an illusion, unless you live in a village where nobody knows you. I live in a small town named Corinth, and it could be the center of creation. Things are still evolving here. This year, I have noticed that most of the citizens are walking on two legs.

My grandmother foretold the future by rolling goat's testicles. She did her readings on a flat surface, and always made sure the testicles were dehydrated. She never told me how I would end up living in Corinth, but maybe she didn't want to destroy my hope.

I have often thought about moving, but something always holds me here. It could be the parole officer, or the fact it's normal to have sex with your cousins in this community. Sex is improved when you are really familiar with the other person.

There are some famous people living in Corinth, but I have not had the opportunity to meet them.

From my kitchen window the town lights are visible, but after 10p.m. the village shuts down, like my boss when she faces a difficult situation at work. I'm not sure what my supervisor actually does to earn a pay-check. There must be a purpose when a dog devours its own shit, but I have no clue what it is.

It would be fun to slip some performance enhancing drugs into my boss's coffee. Only the benign ones, I remain humane. It's my hope to be employed at a library someday.

Corinth does not have a public library, there's no need, the town has cable. We also have our own fire department, and this tempts me to start fires in order to test their response time. They are pretty quick for slow people.

Living in a small town is never boring, even though there's nothing to do. It's the only place where someone has offered to sell me meat out of the back of a pick-up truck.

My neighbors burn their garbage in huge metal barrels, and the smell of plastic burning can make you choke. Is this fresh country air?

I live in a small town, and will probably succumb from carcinogens. Will my passing be insignificant?

Thursday

Have you ever wanted to smother a coworker with a pillow?

One of the team members I work with is named Libby. This is not a true statement. Libby doesn't work, she sits on her ass, she makes personal phone calls, and she eats. She manages to get all this accomplished in eight hours, and still have time for breaks. Libby should be a CEO.

As medical technicians we have the same job title, but the levels of performance are not equal. Sometimes, you can tolerate a slacker, but she's not even pleasant to the eye.

This morning I sent an e-mail to one of my few friends. I explained how working with Libby was like having oral sex with a midget. There's an inordinate amount of work performed by one of the individuals.

My friend responded by suggesting I use another analogy. He claimed there is a rule that demands any sex should be considered good. I know how to adapt and overcome.

I e-mailed him the following response. Working with Libby is like planting a tree, and then getting struck by lightning... Is like killing yourself, and then waking up the next day... Is like petting your dog, and then realizing you don't own one... Is like winning the lottery, and dying before you get the first check... Is like losing your leg under a train, and never getting to meet the conductor... Is like burying your brother, after a while the shovel gets heavy... Is like being in prison without a can opener... Is like losing a testicle in an accident, when you only had one to begin with... Is like flying to Japan for the Olympics, and then finding out they were held the previous year... Is like driving from New York to Cleveland with DVT... Is like spending four years learning Spanish when you live in Kabul... Is like having a fork stuck in your eye, and you can't remember where you left your glasses.

I watch my e-mail, but so far my friend has not replied.

Friday

Sometimes, you can hear the funniest things on the news. Today, there was a story about how a one-handed man had attempted to rob a local donut shop. The robber managed to escape, which leaves me with many questions.

If you only have one hand, how do you write a note? If you carry a gun in the hand, how do you respond when the counter person tries to deliver the money? Do you ask the worker to stuff the money in your pocket, or pin it to your shirt? How hard can it be to catch a one-handed bandit? Does anybody remember The Fugitive?

I wonder if the thief lost his balance while escaping. He could only grab half as much money as a two-fisted person, which means the robber must have requested large bills. If the donut employee had decided to resist, would the bandit have been disadvantaged? If the thief plays golf, how will the robbery affect his handicap?

The reporter doesn't specify if the man was missing his whole arm, or was blessed with a nub. A nub can be applied as a club, and they are also functional when petting a monkey.

What if the one-handed bandit had wanted a coffee to go? A detective could conjecture, if the robber had a getaway vehicle, it was probably an automatic. The investigator could also assume that the vehicle's directional signals were operational. The thief would be unable to use hand signals.

Will the police order him to raise his hands when they apprehend him? How do you handcuff a one-handed man? Where do you connect the empty cuff? The police could snap it through his belt loop, unless the bandit wears shorts.

Will the police fingerprint his one hand twice? In court, how do you raise your right hand to take the oath if you don't have one? Will the judge hold the man in contempt? Is the bandit covered by the Disabilities Act?

If the robber ends up going to prison, how will he shuffle a deck of cards? How can he balance the scales of justice with one hand?

I have many more questions, but nobody is answering me.

Monday

I have an appointment to see a dermatologist today. My primary care physician wants him to examine my moles.

I arrive for my appointment on time, but still end up waiting. This annoys me. Why do they tell you to get here at a certain time, and they aren't ready? The walls of the waiting room are barren of pictures, and the carpet smells like Burma.

After waiting twenty minutes, an emaciated nurse with white hair escorts me to an exam room. I'm tempted to end her suffering, but my health must precede her need.

The guy who delivers my Chinese food comes into the room, and introduces himself as Dr. Cho. I wonder if his first name is Ah. He's a short man with a skeletal frame, and it makes me wonder if anybody in this office ever eats.

He doesn't appear interested when I inform him about the moles in my yard. When mowing my lawn they scatter, unlike the moles on my back which remain immo-bile. Dr. Cho questions me about the relevance.

He seems moderately arrogant, which forces me to take a moment and calmly explain how all things are in relation to one another. Sometimes an innocuous question can bring us very close to death, and we are not even aware of the danger.

Dr. Cho gapes at me, and I'm tempted to toss a mint into his open mouth. I snap my fingers in front of his face, which brings him out of the daze. He commands me to remove my shirt and pants, as he blinks like a Tourette's patient. Now we are getting someplace.

Walking behind me, Dr. Cho fastidiously examines the moles on my back, and comments to the nurse how they all look normal to him. That's the same thing my fifth grade teacher said, when asked about her class.

Dr. Cho mentions, he also removes tattoos, and this odd statement catches me by surprise. There are no tattoos on my body, they only make it easier for the police to identify you. Maybe this idiot thinks I have twenty moles tattooed on my back.

Dr. Cho steps around to my front, examines my chest, and tells the nurse there's evidence of maculation. I thought it was all caught in the towel. I need to wash up more thoroughly after sex. He pulls out the waistband of my underwear, glances down, and appears awestricken.

He informs the nurse that a mole on my lower belly is atypical, and suggests it should be removed. No shit. My doctor sent me here so this idiot could remove the mole. Does this guy know what he's doing? If there had been utensils nearby, I would have removed his tongue to hang in my cellar.

I consent to allow him to remove the mole at some future date, and request the tissue be returned to me. Dr. Cho explains how the tissue sample needs to be sent to a lab for testing. At this point, I'm really starting to dislike the man, but I remember how he gave me extra soy sauce on my last delivery.

He also suggests using a sun screen, and for thirty dollars, I can pick up a three-ounce bottle from the receptionist. Is this man out of his fucking mind? You can get it cheaper at the supermarket.

Dr. Cho reminds me to stop at the desk to make a follow up appointment for the mole removal, and I'm grateful to be released from his presence.

A twenty dollar co-pay, thirty dollars for the sun screen, and Dr. Cho gets two hundred and twenty-five dollars for an office visit. What a racket this guy has.

In the parking lot, I urinate on the Porsche 911 turbo.

Tuesday

If you have to force yourself to go through the motions of life, are you really living? Putting one foot in front of the other is motion, unless you are inebriated, but is that all there is to life.

I keep waiting for the fireworks to go off, but they never come. It's like having a trazadone boner.

Some things in life don't make any sense. My fingers have started to smell like urine, and I can't understand why. Could it be from slicing the onions?

Some of my fingers are bent at awkward angles, and there's extra skin on my knuckles. Pulling on the skin helps me to relax. It's not as good as the haldol, but it will do in a pinch.

Stretching the surplus skin reminds me of a crow pulling apart the carcass of a rabbit. The crow lowers its beak, and stretches the rabbit's skin until it snaps. The skin on my knuckles does not break loose.

Grabbing a handful of strawberries from the fridge, I squeeze them enough to cause the red juice to run between my fingers. The juice tickles, as it dribbles down my arm and onto the floor. It reminds me of my favorite things, and I wish it was snowing.

Scooter is not around to lick the juice off my fingers. My kitty died on the last weekend in July. She stretched out her back legs, blew out some rancid breath, and passed away. My Aunt Ethel exited the world in the same fashion, except she winked at me just as the Reaper took her.

I fondle my knee, but it's not the same as having my kitty around. Raising my pant leg, I gently stroke the tiny hairs on my kneecap. I pinch the knee, but it doesn't howl like Scooter used to. Some things in life can't be recovered, like the flesh my brother lost in the Christmas fire.

It's been a few years since Ralph has called, and I wonder if the phone will ring. Patience is my virtue, and some things are just meant to be. There would never be bird shit on my windshield, if God had not made gravity.

I smell my fingers again, and they are fruity. Life is good, unless that's your sentence.

Wednesday

This morning it's extremely foggy outside, and this worries me. Sometimes I can't feel my legs, and when this happens, it makes me invisible.

Mary is in the bedroom getting dressed, so we can be on our way to work. A wife is blessed by God, but she can be a tortoise when dressing.

My legs remain numb, but my arms are long enough to rattle the lamp. I use it as a signal to help my wife locate me. She rushes from the bedroom, and instructs me to stop shaking the lamp. I have an instinctive ability to motivate people. Mary makes corrections in my life, but she's more gentle than an eraser.

I reach out to touch her neck as she walks by, but she manages to evade my grip. Suddenly, she appears to be in a rush to get to work, but I don't share her enthusiasm. She tosses me the car keys, and I fail to mention the fog outside. My wife likes surprises. The best surprise she ever received was my early parole.

We make our way methodically to the car, and I quickly turn on the headlights. Visibility is nonexistent in the thick fog. In order to improve my vision, I exit the car and walk into the mist. Mary demands to know my destination. I know she is sticking her head out the car window, but there's no visual affirmation. My wife's shouting is increasing in volume, which assures me there's nothing wrong with my hearing.

Someone grabs my arm, as I'm working up the courage to scream for help. I think the person is dragging me in the general direction of my car. The terrorists have come to small town America.

Panic begins to take hold of me, and despite the cool temperature, I'm sweating. A face materializes out of the fog, and I'm humbled to see its Mary pulling me through the murk. It's a miracle how she was able to pinpoint my location.

After a tedious drive into Saratoga, I drop my wife off at the hospital, and continue on to my workplace. The fog has dissipated by the time I pull into the parking lot.

The morning spins by smoothly, allowing me to hope for a tolerable day, but the afternoon turns into a three-ring circus.

The shit hits the fan right after lunch. A patient from my unit runs outside, and positions himself in the center of a field behind the main building. Instead of meditating, the patient slices his wrists with a disposable razor. A counselor witnessing the suicide attempt calls a code blue. If blood is red then why is the code blue?

As a medical staff member, I'm required to respond to the code in spite of my disinclination. With my Director of Nursing huffing and puffing at my side, I jog toward the field. She is wider than I am, and it makes me wonder why there isn't a red flag in her rear pocket.

Her name is Tina, and she's a thorn in the side of many employees. As we are running, Tina mentions how she hopes there won't be a lot of blood. Apparently, body fluids are an issue she is not able to handle. This is typical RN behavior. I assure her that there's no need to worry, blood is one of my favorite things, as long as it's not mine.

She begins loping along faster, but it's actually more of a waddle trot. For an older woman she has a tremendous amount of agility, and the sweat shining on the back of her neck makes her quite attractive. Her buttocks however, could use a little work.

The patient is being restrained by two counselors when we arrive at the field. This allows me to do a rapid assessment of his wrists, and I'm not impressed. I see more blood every morning on my toilet paper. Slicing your wrists is so ordinary.

Most self destructive people seem to lack inventiveness. The patient could have stuffed his mouth and nose with grass from the field until he suffocated. That would have been impressive. If you are going to commit suicide, it would be a good idea to put some planning into it.

Better yet, the patient could have taken off all his clothes, climbed a tree and jumped, after waiting for a good sized crowd to gather. If the patient was patient, he could have stalled long enough for a television station to show up before leaping. Despondent people should remain open to new ways of executing their demise.

If the patient had been the least bit inventive, he could have chewed his leg until he reached the femoral artery, and take a big bite. This would have shown a limberness that would command my attention. Self-destructive people need to make use of their imaginations.

This day has turned out to be amusing, like when my grandfather died and we got the kitchen table back.

As the paramedics were strapping the patient onto the stretcher, I whispered some advice into his ear. I suggested, the next time he feels suicidal, wait until it's foggy and then we wouldn't be able to find him.

Some days I feel good about the work I do.

Thursday

If you hug a cripple, does it make you awkward? The Clinical Director where I work has a habit of hugging her employees every morning as soon as she walks onto the unit. This implies that she's terribly lonely, or is secretly patting them down to detect if they are stealing. Where does she buy her shoes?

I observe Debbie as she embraces each employee, and there's no special attention given. Everyone receives an equal allotment of her time.

I question her about why our Director of Nursing never hugs the medical staff. Debbie suggests I ask my Director, and this logical and sensible answer is quite troubling because it emanates from management.

Most of our managers are mildly retarded, and this could be an awakening. I look to the sky, but the only thing revealed is the mold growing between the ceiling tiles. My mind is racing, but I remain speechless. This is the first time in our company's history that a manager has exhibited common sense.

My intuition says boldness is the way to go in this situation. The Nursing Director's name is Tina, but if she had been born a male, they would have named her prick.

As Tina walks onto the unit, I stroll up to her and aggressively request a hug. She appears uncertain, and I pray my lizard stays flaccid. My eyes roam up and down the length her body, lingering on her ankles. Folds of pale skin hang over the sides of her shoes almost touching the floor. It resembles a cow sitting in a go-cart.

I explain about the Clinical Director giving her staff hugs every morning, and mention how the nursing staff feels left out, like a dog sitting on the porch in Canada.

She hesitates, but then loosely embraces me. I clutch onto her body desperately, my head sinks into her bosom, and it allows the fragrance of stale cigars to float up my nostrils. My arms envelop her, and it feels like a two hundred-pound bag of warm cottage cheese. It makes me aroused and nauseated at the same time. This is just like being married.

I inhale the aromas of oranges and lead coming from her hair, and gaze into her washed out blue eyes. They would look great in one of my grape jelly jars.

Clutching the two enormous handfuls of flesh from her back, conjures up a picture of dumplings filled with maggots. Just when it seems like I have a grip, the flesh squiggles away.

Tina manages to jerk away from me, and she can't help but notice my salute. She quickly retreats from the unit. What, no goodbye?

Friday

Skin is flaking copiously off the bottoms of my feet, and I'm concerned about Hansen's disease. Has someone put a curse on me? Will I be ostracized, like a blender?

Several months ago, I began soaking my genitalia in a solution made from the seed of torreya, after learning the Miracle Grow was not effective. I wonder if the compound would help my feet. We need to safeguard the important parts of our bodies.

There's an abundance of skin flakes in the bottoms of my shoes. I empty them out over a newspaper, and the epidermis cascades into a neat little pile. It's too bad Scooter isn't alive to see this. I really miss my kitty.

I can't ask my wife to check my height, she's at work. Will I become a short person if too much skin sloughs off the bottom of my feet? There will no longer be short people, if they are all the same height as me.

Placing a pot of water on the stove, I wait for it to achieve a rolling boil, and dump the skin flakes in while slowly stirring. The mixture starts to take on the appearance of gray mashed potatoes.

Removing the pot from the stove, I bravely taste a small spoonful. It's not bad, but could use a little salt. After adding seasoning, I place the pot inside the refrigerator.

There are red droplets on my shirt, and my eyes feel like they are bleeding. I run to the bathroom, and examine them in the mirror. They look normal, but it doesn't explain how the blood got on my shirt. Sometimes answers are hard to come by.

Every Saturday there's an Anger Worship Workshop in my basement. I have invited people to attend the Workshop for years, but nobody ever shows up. Some people need to be forced into getting help. Intervention works.

The day has flown by, and I need to pick up Mary from work. Before driving anywhere, I perform a safety check on the vehicle. The tire tread seems to be holding up really well. The way my feet are flaking, it might be a good idea to sew some rubber onto my soles.

After picking Mary up from the hospital, I waste no time hustling home. The more time we spend at the house, the greater the odds of having sex.

After arriving home, I ask Mary if it seems like I'm becoming shorter. She laughs. Her boisterous cackling causes my bladder to scream for release. Running to the bathroom, I hold myself tightly while pissing so that nothing gets away.

When I return to the kitchen, Mary has already started eating dinner. She thanks me for making the mashed potatoes ahead of time.

What a great husband I am.

Saturday

On the news this morning they mentioned civil preparedness. I have no idea what that means, but I trust in evil preparedness.

I need to call my doctors office to get more refills on my lisinopril. They will phone in a refill order to the pharmacy. I am a compliant patient, and my doctor helps me, but the blood pressure medication does not.

My pressure is lower, and my doctor claims it will extend my life, but when my pressure was high, I could ejaculate further. Before starting the medication, I could stand on my deck and knock leaves off the trees, but now all I do is leave a puddle on the railing. Lisinopril cuts into my fun quotient.

I choose my parking spot prudently, I don't want to scratch my door if it becomes necessary to leave quickly. Thankfully, there aren't many cars in the lot.

While waiting for the pharmacist to fill my prescription, I question her about civil preparedness. She spins in my direction, and instructs me to step back in front of the counter. How I ended up behind the counter with a knife in my hand baffles me.

Returning to the customer side of the register, I watch as she scrapes my little white pills into a bottle. The bottle is brown, the pharmacist is white, and the contrast strikes me as peculiar. Trying to adjust the lighting would be impractical, I don't have my sunglasses.

As she looks my way, I attempt to touch my ear with the tip of my tongue, but am not successful. My inability to accomplish this feat is unimportant, it's obvious she's impressed by the attempt. Her eyes are nearly bulging out of her head, as if someone was strangling her.

A voice is whispering in my ear, but there's nobody standing near me. The individual must be invisible, but the air around me isn't shimmering. Why are the cold remedies on the same shelf with the condoms?

The pharmacist hands me my medication, and requests a ten-dollar co-pay. Sweat is pouring down the center of my back, but the knife remains firmly in my grasp. Is this what civil preparedness is all about?

During the drive home, I lick the excess perspiration from my arms. One of my seven knives is missing, and it will need to be replaced.

Sunday

What does it mean when people make the same mistakes over and over?

There's a tall oak tree growing beside my front deck, and the shade from its branches causes unusual shadows to form in the yard. When the shapes change suddenly, they frighten me. When you live in a small town, it's not difficult to discover ways to amuse yourself.

Standing next to the tree, I open a can of white tuna, not dark. The tuna is packed in pure water with no oil. You need to remain conscious of the environment. I pour an ample amount of the water around the base of the tree's trunk.

Looking up and down the street, I can't see any traffic. This could mean the world has ended, and I'm the lone survivor. Who's going to deliver my propane?

Dragging the old wooden ladder from my shed, I lean it upright against the tree. My shed is a small structure, but it contains a great deal of stuff. Some of the treasures hidden inside are useful, like the ladder, while other items are unspeakable. I fondly call it my Helen Keller shed.

My neighbor is watching me from his doorway, and this assures me that life continues onward. Wilbert is a nosey man, but there are days when I appreciate his presence.

He waves at me, and quickly moves in the direction of his garage. Wilbert served in the Navy, which forces him to keep looking over his shoulder. We have been neighbors for 12 years, and that's impressive. The people who previously resided nearby were diagnosed with short life spans, and it's not been determined if the deaths can be attributed to their well water.

I begin climbing up the ladder with the can of tuna held firmly in one hand. Approximately twenty feet from the ground, there's a notch between two branches, where I gently nestle the tin container.

Looking down, the grass seems to undulate, and it

makes me dizzy. I should have worn my safety harness. I climb down cautiously, while hanging onto the ladder for dear life.

I place a can of tuna in this tree once every month, and the results are always the same. By noon time, there's a large yellow cat howling in the tree. Cats are curious animals, but not overly intelligent, like some Presidents.

The poor kitty must have ventured up the tree for the tuna, and now it can't get back down. This operation is going require more manpower, so I call Wilbert over to help. He's a reliable neighbor, but sometimes I wonder why God stockpiled all the slow people in my town.

He's able to assess the situation quickly, and I hold the ladder as he climbs to rescue the kitty. When he's approximately halfway to the notch, the ladder begins shaking with a severity that frightens me. My neighbor is screaming for me to stop, but my arms are shaking with a ferocity beyond my control.

Wilbert scrambles up the ladder, and climbs off onto the branch with the kitty. My neighbor is one of the bravest men I have ever known.

I remove the ladder from the tree, and place it inside the shed. Wilbert's skin tone has changed from a pasty gray to a bright shade of crimson, and he appears to be crying. It's difficult for me to be sure, my vision is not accurate at long distances.

When Mary gets home from work, she questions why Wilbert is in the tree, and this causes me to wonder what has provoked her curiosity. I explain how our neighbor and the cat are bird watching, and she seems satisfied with my answer.

My wife often wakes me during the night to complain about hearing strange noises. I usually wonder what guideline she applies to define strange. Despite my lack of interest, I always get up to investigate.

Listening carefully, I can hear a mewing sound that seems to be originating from outside the house. After turning on the porch light, I step out onto the front deck.

The indecorous noise seems to be coming from the branches of the tree. Wilbert is sitting in the notch crying, and the yellow kitty is sleeping in his lap. This would make a wonderful postcard.

I command Wilbert to shut up his whining, and explain how he will be rescued in the morning. Maybe I should call a local television station to film the extrication.

Before returning to my bed, I remind Wilbert to be careful. A fall at his age could be catastrophic.

The rest of the night passes quietly.

Tuesday

The spiders are scurrying up and down my arms, and it's driving me crazy. They don't go past my shoulder where the salt line is. The insects are not visible, but the movements of my arm hairs disclose their positions. This is what happens when you go to the store for a box of cereal.

Just as I walked down the aisle in search of Fruit Loops, the spiders attacked without warning. My doctor has tried to convince me that the spiders are not real. He must be out of his fucking mind, I can feel their minuscule appendages fastening onto my flesh.

The itchiness is maddening, and I won't be able to tolerate much more. Using my left hand, I remove the penny from beneath my tongue, and grasp it securely between two fingers. One penny is always reserved under my tongue, enabling me to savor the pungent flavor of blood throughout the day.

Using the edge of the coin, I scrape the length of both my arms, until they are inflamed. The spiders are terrified of Lincoln's long face, and they waste no time beating a hasty retreat. The penny is stored back under my tongue.

Someone is screaming at the top of their lungs, but I still have all my clothes on. What the hell is happening?

There's a young blond headed child at the far end of

the cereal aisle, and he's yelling and slapping at a middle-aged woman. The lad is addressing the dour woman as mom, interspersed with profanities. Who is the parent in this situation?

The boy continues his tantrum, wailing and stomping his feet like a televangelist. I yearn to stuff his mouth full of Captain Crunch, so I can watch him choke.

Why is there no discipline in families anymore? The mother should drag the little bastard out into the parking lot, and put a cigar out on the back of his neck. This technique may seem brutal, but the results speak for themselves.

After the child gets older, he can visit a tattoo artist and have the burn altered into a cyclops. In order to avoid making the one-eyed creature appear unbalanced, you need to center the fiery cigar exactly. Most children have small heads, which allows you to hold them steady.

Cigar discipline also works as a deterrent for smoking. Bad habits are easy to avoid when you are motivated. My son has never smoked.

If the child ever forgets and acts bad in the store again, you simply slide a cigar half way out of your pocket. It works like magic. Discipline is a necessary tool, but you need to remain alert for the anger misdirected back at you.

I fondly recollect how my father taught me the multiplication tables. When my answer was wrong, dad would delicately squeeze my fingers with a pair of pliers. Dad was a mechanic, and he always brought his tools home with him. One of my fingers is shaped exactly like the Mississippi River near Memphis.

My father got his exercise by holding me around the ankles, and pounding my head into the floor. We were a low income family so the carpet was not very thick. He turned my world upside down, and it would make him proud to see how his creation turned out.

The lady and her unruly child have gone about their business, permitting me to mind mine. Grabbing a box of Fruit Loops from the shelf, I checkout without incident.

After arriving home, I place the cereal on the kitchen

table. I will ask Mary to open it when she gets home, in case there are spiders inside.

Wednesday

There's a time in everyone's life when they reach a fork in the road. A decision has to be made on which way to turn, and each person must determine their own direction. I find these decisions tine tingling.

Choose one way, and life continues as you know it, choose the other direction, and discover sudden death. It astonishes me how some people don't realize when they have reached the fork in the road. One word, or one movement could send them in the wrong direction, yet they remain unaware.

Some people will never comprehend how close they have come to greeting death, but I know.

It's October, and time for the baseball playoffs to begin. It's also the beginning of hunting season. These two events may seem incongruous, but they are not. I will never pursue an animal when hunting, they are God's precious creatures, and should not be harmed by man. Animal fur is comforting when you rub it on certain areas of your body.

The warm-blooded species which I pursue can be terminated with a baseball bat. Wood not aluminum. It's important to respect tradition. Hunting season and baseball arrive together in a blessed way.

My hunt begins by identifying my prey's mode of transportation. This particular victim owns an old green Ford truck, and those types of vehicles are easier to trail than cars. God has blessed me with the ability to be extremely quiet during tracking. My dad always said, I would never be a leader, but I can sure follow.

My victim will never hear me coming, unless I want him to. There could be some hearing impaired people buried in my yard.

The creature in the green truck stops at the same beverage shop every morning to get his coffee. The patterns in life are what lead to our demise. You should never leave the house at the same time every morning, or drive the same route to work. Change is essential to survival.

I follow my quarry to his hovel, and park across the street to observe his movements. I wait and watch, and watch and wait. A good hunter must be patient, and search for patterns, like the squares in my grandmother's quilts.

Specifically, I watch for night patterns. Hunting during daylight would be wonderful, but some people might find my actions disturbing or distasteful. Being a good citizen, I consider my activity an invigorating part of community service.

After stalking him for two weeks, there are notations of my victim's movements in my memory. People are oblivious of their surroundings, like an old woman leaning over a balcony.

My prey has a habit of bringing out his garbage every Wednesday at 5a.m. The garbage man arrives to pick it up at 7a.m. I admire people who can stay ahead of schedule.

While patiently waiting for the night to arrive, I rub my bat with extra virgin olive oil. Slip slide, slip slide.

Wednesday at 4a.m., I park two blocks away from my victims dwelling. This is the perfect distance for a hunter. Next comes the downtime, which is something I have plenty of experience at. I waited seven years in prison to get paroled, I waited forty minutes at Disneyland to get on a ride, and I have been waiting fifty years for my father to die.

I lick the bat handle to assist in securing my grip. This is not the moment to strike out. I visualize a home run.

I begin strolling down the street a little before 5a.m. I cruise smooth and easy, like yogurt without the fruit.

My target is placing his garbage at the curb, inattentive of his surroundings. Just as he turns his head to look in my direction, I swing the bat, and its candy cane rain. I would love to witness the droplets in sunlight, but my work must be done during darkness.

This is turning out to be a great baseball morning, and it looks like this one got smacked out of the park. Sometimes your target will spasm or twitch, but this guy is not moving at all.

I check the carotid pulse, a professional hunter should never let his prey suffer. There's nothing to snap my fingers to, as I begin folding my trophy into one of the large black bags we hunters use. The street is quiet during my labor, and I permit myself a moment to absorb the tranquility of the neighborhood, while knotting the bag securely.

The garbage man will have one extra trash bag this morning, and I hope he doesn't charge by weight. It makes no sense to put a financial burden on other people.

It's so peaceful in this place, I find myself wishing to stay longer, but it's not meant to be. Hunting can be tiring, and you need to be aware of your bodies need for rest.

Upon arriving home, I start a huge bonfire in my backyard. I really liked those sneakers, but the marshmallows help me forget.

The following day, while punching the time clock at work, I smile to myself.

Soon there will be a job opening posted.

Thursday

The sky is full of puffy white clouds, and I enjoy trying to discover faces in the shapes. It's too bad the clouds are not red.

I skip to the car, knowing the erratic movement will cause the snipers to miss. Gunmen are always out there, and there are bullet holes in my yard to prove it. Moles dwell in the holes, and due to the assassins poor marksmanship, my yard has become a habitat for many wild things.

After ducking inside my car, I quickly back out of the driveway, and journey down the road with no specific destination in mind. I like to drive, and see where God leads me.

The breeze ruffles the fine hairs on my wrist, as I hang my left arm out the window. It conjures up an image of playing dominos with a naked Chinese lady. Things jiggle each time she slams a domino on the table.

My hands never slip off the steering wheel when they are clean, and this allows me to drive above the speed limit.

While racing around a blind corner, I become aware of a man standing close to the edge of the road. He appears to be looking in his mailbox, and he nearly collides with my car. His clumsiness irritates me. In the rear view mirror, I notice he has become coordinated enough to shake his fist in my direction.

I don't approve of people who gesticulate in public. That should be done in the privacy of your own home.

Parking along the shoulder of the road, I take a deep breath and slide the knife out from under my seat. While holding the weapon out of sight, I stroll toward the red-faced man. He's jumping up and down in his driveway, screaming obscenities in my general direction, and it makes me believe he wants to play. This looks like the first exercise he has attempted in a while.

As I dash forward with the knife in my hand, he spins around and sprints toward his house. The man has dropped some mail on the ground, and I wonder if this is part of the game. My elevator of pain is going up, but there's not enough privacy in this neighborhood for him to fully appreciate the ride.

I scoop the loose mail off the ground, and transport it back to my car. There's a siren wailing in the distance, but thanks to aversion therapy, it's a sound I can recognize and evade.

I drive away from the area faster than a priest can hide his pecker. After arriving at my house, I peruse the envelopes scattered across the passenger seat. There are four letters addressed to someone named Simon Brown. It's puzzling how Mr. Brown's mail ended up in my car.

As a youngster, solving puzzles was one of the few things that came easy for me. Fetching the gas can from my shed, I pour a tiny amount of fuel over the letters and light them up. The problem is solved.

Fire is a cleansing agent, and my soul is spotless. The only thing missing is a stick and marshmallows. Ashes to ashes, dust to dust.

In a few weeks, I will leave a present for Mr. Brown in his mailbox. I hope he has a strong stomach.

Friday

Getting old sucks, and these days it can be even worse if you eat your spinach. They are having a country wide recall on the vegetable due to e-coli contamination. I'm pretty sure mom didn't have this in mind when she told me to eat my vegetables. Old age is rough, but bloody diarrhea is worse.

Apparently, the problem spinach originated from California. Thanks to my fathers migrant nature, we lived in California for a while, and I have seen the spinach fields stretching as far as the eye can see. The large farms hire hundreds of migrant workers to harvest the spinach, and they work extended hours under the blistering sun. I have never observed any toilets in the area. What causes e-coli?

If you have varicose veins in your legs, you should never ingest vegetables with veins in the leaves. It can cause cross contamination.

The veins in my legs are blue, the blood flowing through them is red, and my skin is white. I resemble the American flag when lying naked on the bed.

A few of my veins bulge, and the one behind my right knee looks like a huge blue knot. The veins in my legs diverge, which makes it difficult to read the written message. Are my veins full of ink?

My grandmother had wicked varicose veins in her

legs, even though her thighs and calves were quite voluptu-
ous. My parents used her as a babysitter for my brother and
me. By the time I was eight years old, it wasn't necessary for
anyone to watch me. There isn't much need for a babysitter
after you have killed your first human. That's written
somewhere in the common sense book of rules.

Before her services were no longer needed, I used to
pinch the veins running down the backs of grandmas' legs
until she screamed for mercy. Years later, I would experience an orgasm while someone was screaming.

Grandmas' veins were as thick as my pinkie finger,
and it made me thirst to bite them, but my hunger was curbed
by wisdom. Her feet had turned black from lack of circula-
tion, by the time Mr. Reaper came for her. Integration came
to her doorstep, whether she liked it or not.

She always kept raisins in her pocket, and when we
behaved, she would dole out a few. She gave me a whole
handful to stop squeezing her leg.

When she died, it was three days before they found
her body, and she was covered with ants. The insects were
her final accouterments.

At grandmas' funeral, I was forced to stand on my
toes in order to see inside the casket, but it's the extra effort
put forth in life that reaps rewards.

My grandmother looked like she was sleeping, but I
swear she opened one eye and winked at me. As a sign of
respect, I grazed my tongue along the edge of the casket until
my father pulled me away.

Getting old sucks, and so did my father.

I hope he eats his spinach.

Saturday

On the news this morning, they mentioned that the
numbers of violent crimes in New York State are increasing.
As a concerned citizen, this worries me.

When I look out my living room window, I don't see any bodies lying in the street. I open the window expecting to be greeted by the tortured screams of victims, but there's only the clamor of birds chirping. Where's this increase of violence they were talking about?

Curiosity causes me to walk next door, and knock on my neighbor's door. Wilbert is an honest man, and I'm hoping he can answer my questions about increased crime. There are days when the voices suggest eliminating him, but the command has not been issued.

My neighbor hesitantly opens his door, and there are no obvious injuries to his person. I question him about being violently assaulted recently. He shakes his head negatively, as tears stream down his cheeks. This man is close to having some kind of breakdown, and he's far too emotional. I wave goodbye, and walk back to my house.

My investigation into elevated violence will have to be continued at a later time. I have an appointment to get my oil changed today.

Grabbing my keys off the counter, I sprint to the car, while constantly glancing over my shoulder. I have found no evidence of a violent crime wave, but nevertheless I remain attentive.

My drive to the service station is uneventful, but I notice the name has been changed from Mobil to Exxon. Aren't they the same thing? It's like saying feces instead of shit.

Entering the station, I endeavor not to appear confused by the name change. The regular counter guy is not here, and this irregularity does not go unnoticed. I wonder what this jerk has done with Dave. The new guy looks like an anorexic Homer Simpson, and when I hand him my keys something moves in my stomach.

Jim is my personal mechanic, and he has shown up for work today. Nobody else has ever touched my cars private parts. It makes me feel protected.

Jim spends the majority his day in the garage bays, and the only time he makes an appearance is when he delivers the bill. He seems like a great guy, except for one thing. He always wears white socks, which clash with his shirt. You should always be color coordinated before leaving the house. In spite of all his faults, Jim knows enough to save my dirty oil. He pours it inside the plastic jugs behind my front seat. It's all about the service, and that's how they keep me coming here.

I take a seat in the waiting area, while Jim labors on my car. Homer is standing behind the counter picking his nose. Where do they find these people? The station offers free coffee to their customers, but I never accept. This is New York State, and nothing is really free.

There's a yellow sign stuck on the door leading into the garage bays, and it reads Unauthorized Personnel Not Allowed Past This Point. What aptitude test permits you to be authorized?

On previous visits, I have witnessed Dave entering this door, so he must be authorized. On several of those occasions, I have tried without success to peer over his shoulder. What's going on back there?

What's the big secret? Are they performing unnatural acts on my car? There are no answers because my car can't speak. This also means my vehicle can't testify about the things it has seen me do.

Jim bounces through the yellow signed door with my invoice, and informs me the car is all set. All set for what? Why do some people think they have to speak in code, when there aren't any Navajos around?

He presents the bill to the mystery cashier, and leaves to pull my car around front. Does this place have great service or what? After paying Homer, I step outside just as Jim is parking my car. If I could go back in time, it would be to this happy moment before my mechanic's day went all wrong.

Jim is climbing out of the car, but before he can pass me the keys, they drop from his hand and fall under the front seat. This is not good news for my favorite mechanic.

He bends over, and after searching under the seat, retrieves the keys and hands them to me. Jim has viewed something beyond his understanding, and his saucer sized eyes bear witness. It's like a voter peering inside the President's ear.

Beneath the driver's seat are two items for my eyes only, and it's too bad Jim saw them. The knife is mine, the cereal bowl belongs to Mary.

Jim encourages me to have a great day, and attempts to escape into the safe zone within the garage bays. Calmly, I command him to get inside the car, and ride shotgun with me to the corner, just to be sure the vehicle is operating properly. The car is running like a Swiss watch, and it proves Jim is a superb mechanic.

While watching the evening news, I happen to catch a story about a local mechanic being murdered. The video is shocking as the camera stays focused on the victim's blood soaked white socks.

I guess violent crime is on the rise.

Sunday

As old age creeps up on me, I find the memories of my youth are fading away, like the President's approval ratings. There are times I can't even remember what my brother looks like. There are no pictures of Ralph to refresh my memory, they were all lost in the Christmas fire.

I'm sure my brother does not resemble me, but I check in the mirror anyway. We have not seen or spoken to each other in many years. This was his choice, not mine.

Ralph lives somewhere in Florida, but he keeps changing his address. It's a big state. There are people who could track my brother down, but it would detract from the mystery.

My brother has physical scars, mine are all mental, except for the burns on my legs, and the extension cord welts on my shoulders. I miss my brother so much it causes my stomach to burn, but Tums help.

Despite my failing memory, I can still fondly recall playing marbles with my brother in our backyard. The summer sun would warm our necks, as we hunched over the sandy soil, smacking the glass orbs together. When they smashed against each other, the solid crack sounded like you were breaking some camels back with a sledge hammer.

Ralph always ended up with more marbles, and his mocking laughter would ring in my ears for days. Justice was served when my brother got a bee stuck in his ear. He spent a lot of time screaming during his youth.

At the age of fifty-five, I have no marbles left. It's not like I lost them, or can't find them, but you can't even buy them anymore. In life you must learn to adapt, adjust, and overcome.

Obstacles only lead to more adventures, and this brings me to strangling rabbits.

Living in the country has its benefits, it just takes longer to find them. There are always plenty of bunnies in the yard. When you squeeze their furry necks tightly, the shiny eyes bulge from their skulls. This evokes images of the marbles I had as a child.

You need to remain safety conscious at all times, in case the bunnies try to bite. They have large square teeth. The only disappointment is my inability to apply enough pressure to make the eyes pop entirely from their heads.

Sometimes, you have to be willing to accept that your childhood is gone forever. At least I can still remember some of the good times.

Monday

My parents always suggested that there was something wrong with me. When I pissed in the yard this morning, tiny black flies dove into the urine and flew away. They seemed to come out of nowhere, just like a car salesman.

I urinate in the backyard once a day, in order to aerate my private parts. During the winter months this activity can be invigorating and humbling.

The black flies were willing to dive into my urine, but they would not approach me. This could be a sign from God. Maybe I am dying. Something tells me this is not going to be a good day. It's like when a hostage taker tells the negotiator to send in condoms.

I should have eased up on the coffee this morning because my bladder is full again. There are no flies in my bathroom as I urinate.

This whole situation is making me nervous, and I need to find a way to relax. When my kitty was alive, I could remain calm by stroking her back. Scooter has passed away, leaving me to fondle myself.

Running to the kitchen, I remove one of the cow eyes from the freezer. They are individually sealed in zip lock bags, and they can't blink anymore.

Once the eye is partially defrosted, it makes an excellent stress ball. The trick is to get just the right amount of thawing or it gets messy.

Holding a frozen eye against my privates enables me to travel in public without frightening people. This is only necessary when I become pendulous.

After squeezing the cow eye for several minutes, I begin to realize there's nothing wrong with me after all.

Thursday

Today, the growth will be removed from my left side. My primary care physician noticed the lump during a routine visit, after I called his attention to it. Dr. Knopp was concerned because the mass had appeared and grown so rapidly.

One month ago, I noticed the swelling while admiring my naked body in the mirror. It started as a nickle sized red induration on Labor Day, and it was beginning to look like my brother's head by Veterans Day.

After heating a butter knife on the stove, I touched the growth briefly in order to teach it a lesson. The mass did not scream, proving it was not my brother. It's amazing how hot a butter knife can get.

During my exam with Dr. Knopp, I explained how a cow had nuzzled me in the area as a child. He informed me the animal groping would not have caused the condition, and suggested I see a specialist named Dr. Rajec.

Suggestions can be welcome events, unless they are offered in a men's room. I took my physicians advise, and Dr. Rajec has scheduled my surgery for this morning.

Regular doctors will send you to specialists when they don't know what else to do. My growth is now the size of a townhouse cracker. The wheat ones, not the original.

I considered leaving the lump alone to see how big it would get, but Mary started complaining about it causing her discomfort. Before we went to bed every night, I would squeeze the growth, and force it to wink at her. Her sense of humor is not as expansive as mine.

Mary is by my side, as we walk into the surgeon's office in downtown Saratoga. I should ask why they aren't performing the operation in a hospital. Am I receiving substandard treatment? I instruct my wife not to sign any papers that mention donating organs.

When I hold my hand over the growth, heat radiates right through my shirt.

After checking in with the receptionist, I take a seat in the waiting area. Leaning over the side of the chair, I yank up a pinch of fabric from the carpet and smell it. Mary slaps my hand away from my face, and tells me to stop. Does she think I'm a child?

My opportunity to retaliate is stolen away by the nurse calling my name. Before taking one step down the hallway to meet this woman, I remind my wife of what happened to Jimmy Hoffa. Mary encourages me to move with a light push to the center of my back.

The nurse, who seems more agreeable than my wife, escorts me to a small exam room, but does not hold my hand on the journey. Her name tag reads Celia, but that can't be correct. As soon as she exits the room, I inspect the corners for wolves, but dust balls are the only visible wildlife. This means there will be a famine this year.

The woman who is impersonating Celia returns and instructs me to remove my shirt, and lie on the table. This sounds like it could become interesting. A cannibal has never missed a meal, and I never miss an opportunity.

Dr. Rajec makes an appearance, and wants to know how I'm doing. He's a short rotund man, who reminds me of the Pillsbury Doughboy after a visit to India. I respond by telling him my tumor is having a very bad day. He smiles, and I wonder what's wrong with his teeth.

The doctor draws a circle around my growth with a blue marker, and now it looks like Maui. He explains how the nurse will numb the area with a shot of lidocaine, and instructs me to relax. As he exits the room, I'm concerned about my wife's safety.

The nurse is warning me about feeling a little prick, and this opens the door to many responses from me, but I offer none. Could the lump have been caused by tying my shoes too tight?

There's a huge overhead light shining down on my side, but I don't hear the train coming. Dr. Rajec has reappeared, like a magician, and he questions my readiness. After assuring him of my preparedness, he begins the operation.

This guy wastes no time cutting, and out of respect for the growths privacy, I don't look. There isn't any pain, and this disappoints me, but there's a sensation of warm liquid trickling down my side. I hope it's blood.

The doctor wants to know how I'm doing, and I'm thinking he should be answering that question. He's wearing a yellow mask over the lower portion of his chubby face. Using one hand, I remove the wallet from my pants pocket, and offer it to him.

During a robbery your money is never worth your life, unless there's more than ten dollars in your wallet. Dr. Rajec instructs me to put the wallet away, and lie still. Something about this man makes me uneasy.

He instructs the nurse to cauterize the wound, and I feel the sensation of heat, but no pain. This astonishes me, and I question if anyone else can smell pork chops cooking. Dr. Rajec laughs through his mask, and despite my earlier reservations, I'm beginning to like this guy.

He begins sewing me up, and each time he pulls tight a stitch, I pinch his pudgy leg. The doctor moves beyond my reach, and finishes the sutures. He instructs the nurse to finish up, and place a dressing on the wound. How the hell did I get wounded in the doctor's office?

Dr. Rajec leaves the exam room without even saying goodbye, but maybe we will meet again. I raise my head from the table to look at the sutures, and they remind me of the stitches on a baseball. Maybe the surgeon knew my father.

Celia completes the dressing, and reminds me to stop at the receptionist to make an appointment to have the sutures removed in two weeks.

There's nothing more comforting than to see your wife's smiling face waiting for you after a near death experience.

I see a tragopan on the drive home, which means this year's famine will be mild.

Saturday

Autumn is here, and the season of despair will be next. I enjoy the fall because it starts the football season, and the cold weather causes people to huddle.

The back of my brothers head is shaped exactly like a football. Its regulation size, and a great deal of labor went into forming it. I'm not a slacker. I wonder if Ralph really appreciates all the time and effort that went into molding his skull.

There's a method to shaping a child's noggin in a vice. You must start when they are very young, and be extremely meticulous. Tightening the vice just the right amount requires a tremendous degree of skill. I am a tradesman. Too much pressure applied, and you make a mess on the work bench.

As I was growing up, our family moved back and forth across the country every few years. The moves were usually precipitated by my father noticing one of the neighbor's kids were missing. My father never missed much, especially when he was throwing a baseball.

Fall is also the season when the leaves change colors in the Northeast. My neighbors do not, they remain a dull ashy gray. Caucasians are pretty much without color, unless you hold them tightly around the throat. This can make them turn red or blue. White folks are patriotic, but the leaves are more intriguing.

The green foliage will change to brilliant reds, oranges, and yellows. It's like a deluge of blood flowing before my eyes, and I beg God not to turn off the tap. As a sensitive man, I'm fully capable of appreciating the beauty of nature.

Standing on my deck allows me to observe the many colors up close, and it leaves me in awe of God's majestic creation. Because awe should only be guided in one direction, I remain fully clothed.

The soft breeze is knocking the leaves loose from the branches, and they flutter to the ground. Some of them land near my feet. I attempt to pluck a few of the leaves from the air, without much success. As a Caucasian, I generally lack coordination.

The leaves are like a monster kaleidoscope drifting in front of me. It releases a violent urge to scrape out my own eyes, I'm not worthy to observe such beauty. The destructive urge passes quickly, like gas from a burrito.

I manage to snatch one of the red leaves from the air, stuff it into my mouth and swallow. Fiber is beneficial, and it's important to be aware of your nutritional needs.

In a few weeks, the trees will be barren of leaves, the sky will be gray and dreary, and the chill of winter will be upon us. Once the snow arrives, I will explore the woods behind my house for frozen things.

Monday

I knew today was going to be a special day, as soon as I opened my eyes.

There have been memorable days in my past, when I would wake up in a hotel covered with blood. The open window had caused the body fluids to caramelize, and it made me crave waffles. Today, is going to be that kind of day.

This morning, I woke up in my own bed with my wife sleeping soundly beside me. I touched one of her nipples, but she did not respond. I lapped the drool from the side of her face, but she snoozed onward. Thank God for sedatives.

My right foot was stuck to the bed sheet, and there was a damp sock under my pillow. I yanked my foot loose from the sheet and sat up on the side of the bed, being careful not to let my penis drag on the floor.

Now I'm sitting on the edge of the bed, while Mary continues to snore. My wife is off today, but I need to get my ass ready for work.

I ease the blanket off my wife in order to check for scorpions. After performing a semi-cavity check, she seems clear of critters, and I toss the covers back on top of her.

I briskly wash my vital areas, throw on some clothes, and hustle out the door. There's enough trouble awaiting me at work, without my adding to it by punching in late.

Last weekend, I refused to be mandated to work a double shift. This morning, my Director of Nursing will call me into her office and discipline me. This has been the pattern of Tina's reactionary tactics in the past.

I have explained to my supervisors that mandation is unacceptable, but I will tolerate termination. They seem to think I'm not serious about this issue, but they are sadly mistaken. Mandating people is like slavery, without the food and sexual favors.

Pulling into the parking lot, I'm three minutes early for my shift. While punching in, I fondle the time clock in the area where plastic meets metal. This could be our last day together. There's an emptiness inside me, except for where the worms are.

Just before lunch, the Director of Nursing calls me to her office, and tells me to bring a union steward. Tina is wired, but not too tight. Taking a union steward to a disciplinary meeting is like sucking on a mint as the tsunami rolls over you. Your breath will be fresh as you drown.

Tina prefers to sit in front of her desk, in order to intimidate people. She looks like a rhino piled into a lawn chair. If she had remained behind the large oak desk, I may have been able to trap her. I slide the visitor chair from the corner, and place it beside her. As I sit, I can't help but wonder if she's aware of my fondness for her.

Without offering any beverages, she begins lecturing me in that monotone voice her husband must adore. After about two seconds of that shit, my mind closes for renovations.

I can't stop staring at the sheen of sweat coating Tina's calves, as she rocks back and forth in the leather chair. The glistening hairs on her legs call my name, and I wonder if she will properly introduce us. The faint yeasty odor of bread dough drifts through the air each time she rocks back in the chair, but I don't recall seeing a bakery nearby.

Each time Tina rolls forward in the chair, her pendulous breasts flop to the side, and I wait eagerly to see which one will get trapped in her armpit. The pallid breasts flopping around elicit the image of a leper attempting to tread water.

Tina questions me if I understand what she's saying, but my attention has been elsewhere. I resign my position, and give her my two-week notice. She's becoming visibly angry, not because I'm quitting, but because the meeting did not finish with her on top.

Why does it have to be a two-week notice? Who made the decision about the proper length of time?

After vacating Tina's office, I feel a great sense of freedom and anticipation. My testicles sing a song of joy.

I knew today was going to be momentous.

Friday

Work is not a burden, it's a blessing, but when I was employed it didn't seem that way. It's been one month since I left my job, and opportunities are transitory. It seems like nobody wants to hire a convict.

Should I have considered this possibility before leaving my job? There's no going backwards, my mind has no reverse gear, fast forward is the only way to go.

I spend my days wandering the malls, looking for easy targets. It may be time to take my show on the road, before my hunger increases.

There comes a time in everyone's life when they need to make some changes. It's time to spread my wings, and relocate to the blistering sun of Arizona, leaving the cold dreariness of New York behind. Cross country trips can be stimulating, and are usually abounding with opportunities.

The car is stuffed with our worldly goods, and Mary has swallowed enough sedatives to make her comfortable during the extended trip.

As I was carrying my wife to the car, it didn't take long to realize, she had packed on a few extra pounds. Nothing to eat for the next three days should remedy that.

Wednesday

Mary is coming to life in the back seat, and questioning me about where we are. That's a tough question, and at the moment, I'm more concerned about how the blood got smeared on my shirt.

The last road sign read, Phoenix 100 miles.

Tuesday

Mary and I are beginning to get comfortable in Arizona. It's been a relief to escape from New York, and all the investigations. We are going to love living in the Southwest. Searching for apartments and employment can be exhausting, and you need to take some time to relax.

We decided to take a break, and go hiking in Cochise Canyon. It used to be the stronghold of some Indian, but I can't remember his name.

After hiking into the desert for one mile we came across a large orange sign posted alongside the trail. My experiences in life have taught me that orange signs usually do not bear good news.

The sign read, Danger-High Mountain Lion Activity-Proceed At Your Own Risk. Never having been able to resist a challenge, we proceeded down the trail.

I'm thinking, how big are these animals, maybe 20 to 30 pounds. A couple of well-placed kicks, and a mountain lion will be hauling ass away from me. Mary did not seem reassured, but the hike was uneventful.

After returning to the visitor center, I questioned one of the park rangers about the mountain lions. Imagine my amazement when he informed me the lions had been stalking hikers during daylight hours, and should be considered extremely dangerous.

He also explained how the cats can be nine feet in

length, and weigh up to 275 pounds. The ranger suggested, if attacked never turn my back or run because it triggers the animals chase instinct. What the fuck. He also recommended striving to remain on my feet.

As if this wasn't enough, the gleeful ranger continued with his wildlife information seminar. He stated the cats are solid muscle, can leap 20 feet and outrun a deer. This made me understand, if attacked my ability to maintain an upright position might be problematic.

That night I slept well, and did not scratch myself.

The following afternoon, Mary and I returned to Cochise Canyon which looked the same as when we left it. Again, one mile down the trail the mountain lion dangers sign was posted. The hike beyond this point is a steep incline, which challenged me to pick up the pace. Mary seemed to be wheezing a bit, and had fallen back behind me. I estimated the distance to be approximately 20 feet. So far, so good.

I remained diligent, watching the brush and over-hanging cliffs, but witnessed no movement. My wife continued to struggle with the pace, and before long was bent over beside the trail drinking water. I encouraged her to hurry and catch up because that's what good husbands do.

From my vantage point, I was able to observe both sides of the trail as Mary climbed to join me. There was no movement other than a few rabbits and lizards. This enabled me to conclude the mountain lion warning was concocted.

After we both made it to the crest of the ridge, I noticed it was getting dark. My observation skills are heightened after Mary points things out to me. Hiking after dark in Arizona is not against the law, but it's not recommended.

I am always prepared, like ready-made crust. Inside my backpack there is a flashlight, two bottles of water, and a tube of lubricant. Before leaving the house, I also tucked one half of a bologna sandwich inside my sock in case of an emergency.

Hiking back down the canyon at night allowed us to hear many types of noises, and they were all disconcerting. Some of the commotion was caused by my wife stumbling around in the dark.

She remained in close proximity which made me very horny. The ravines were extremely steep, and I was prepared for casualties.

Halfway down the canyon, I flipped off the flashlight, pulled down my pants, and asked Mary if she could see me. Sometimes after a few drinks, I shine. She ignored my question, and firmly instructed me to turn on the light.

Clicking the light back on, it appeared as if live shadows were slinking back into the surrounding desert. Swinging the flashlight in a wide arc, enabled me to see eyes reflected in the beam. There was a rustling noise originating from the nearby brush.

There are people in this world who do not understand how to have fun, but I'm not one of them. Switching off the flashlight once more, a loud grunting noise erupted to my left, followed by what felt like a small child with spiked hair brushing against my leg.

Mary screamed, and upon hearing her, my first thought was, my God this is fun. On, off, on, off with the light until Mary slapped me. An obedient husband always responds to violence, usually with retaliation. My reaction was to turn the flashlight back on, and proceed down the canyon.

My wife appeared frightened, and damp in some of her personal areas. I was missing an article of footwear, and a moderate piece of flesh was ripped from my ankle. Astoundingly, I perceived no pain from the wound.

Mary applied a vulgarity to express how we needed to hurry back to the car. I briefly considered making her aware my injury, but as a man I have learned to suffer alone. Empathy sucks. After rubbing some dirt into the wound and shaking it off, we continued our quest to find the car.

We hiked the rest of the way rather quickly considering I was missing a shoe. It's really remarkable how much heat the ground retains after dark.

Moving to Arizona has solved a lot of my disposal problems, and I believe we are going to love living here.

Things desiccate faster in the desert.

Made in the USA
Monee, IL
07 July 2026

56551691R00109